About the Author

G. R. Malowney has been working in various roles in secondary school education for the past twenty years, since graduating from Liverpool Hope University College with a BA Honours in English Literature and Education Studies.

He has always had an interest in true crime and murder mystery literature which probably stemmed from his love of the American TV series *Columbo*.

He is married with three children and lives in Greater Manchester. His hobbies include hiking, playing badminton, table tennis and five-a-side football. He also spends his time creating pen and ink artwork and is an amateur singer/songwriter with a passion for performing.

Scratch the Surface

G. R. Malowney

Scratch the Surface

Olympia Publishers
London

www.olympiapublishers.com
OLYMPIA PAPERBACK EDITION

A CIP catalogue record for this title is
available from the British Library.

ISBN: 978-1-80439-667-4

First Published in 2024

Olympia Publishers
Tallis House
2 Tallis Street
London
EC4Y 0AB

Printed in Great Britain

Dedication

I dedicate this book to my children; Emily, Dylan-James and Georgia-May x

Acknowledgements

Thank you to my wife, Laura, for inspiring me to write this
book.

Year 1968

Prologue
Action Man

The young boy's chest wheezed as he struggled to catch his breath. He stopped for a brief second and tugged on his light blue inhaler. Both muddy legs throbbed as they continued to carry his already weary body through the cut-up football field. Despite his best efforts, he failed to dodge any of the large buckshot pellets of rainwater that exploded all around him. Leaving the field behind, he headed towards the rain soaked, drab street with its array of bargain shops, a sawdust covered butcher's shop and a rather out of place ornate Victorian bank.

The deluge had already drenched the once dusty pavements and battered the red tiled roofs. The rainwater had collected at the side of the road before it gargled and disappeared down the thirsty expectant drain. After all, rain is no stranger to Greater Manchester and this Northern city certainly got its fair share. On this particular day however, the grey clouds had gathered without warning, above the green hills and dropped their load on the small town of Oldham. This part of Oldham was a place well known for not being classy. It was the kind of place that one would always be passing through, as to stay for any amount of time may corrupt one's character or infect a visitor somehow.

Above the line of shops on the high street were several grim, poky flats with dirty greasy windows and behind one of these now sat the boy who wore a tight-fitting T-shirt with a colourful photo of *Batman & Robin* springing into action on it.

He sat idyll and looked out on to a drizzly grey scene from his box bedroom on the first-floor just above the local sandwich shop 'Fresh Bite'. This sounded great in principle with all the aromas of frying bacon and fresh ingredients but in reality, the smell of food frying was masked by the overflowing rubbish black bags with pungent rotting meat lying in its own bin juice that lay just outside the back door attracting curious cats and rummaging rats.

Although surrounded by fields unfortunately, greenery could not be seen from his vantage point, only the occasional car that braved the weather and sprayed a fine mist across the length of the road. The heavy grey clouds had completely blocked out any remnants of blue sky. As anyone who has lived in England knows that the six-week summer holidays were never a guarantee of sunny weather, not even a half-decent one.

The heavens had opened on him when he was only five minutes from home, but that was enough time to completely soak him like a drowned rat. He had contemplated standing underneath the 237 bus shelter and wait for the worst of the weather to pass, but that would have been a whole afternoon stood outside in his Oldham Athletic shorts, boots and his navy-blue woollen jumper with its small owl and Latin scroll insignia that he also needed for school.

When at home, he knew to stay in his bedroom and not interrupt his mother when she was working. He had learnt to tune out of the occasional moan and the more than frequent raised voice or sudden thud. He didn't know what his mum did for work but he knew that Mummy was never alone or lonely because men were always turning up at all hours. Sometimes they would turn up just before he dropped off to sleep, sometimes waking him up in the middle of the night or when he came back from school and having his tea. Men were always around. Just like Mr Patel who ran the sweet-smelling corner shop 'Patel's News', 'Creepy Baz', and 'Old Man Fred' who cleaned the windows of the bank. It's funny really, they were always coming around here but would never say hello to him when they saw him playing out or knocking for his friends.

Carefully he spread his navy-blue jumper which, regrettably, had soaked up the majority of the sudden downpour on the clothes maiden, which was already covered in washing. With hindsight maybe, he should have wrung the Jumper out a little more because it produced its own little downpour on the black and white lino in the kitchen.

He dived down on the worn-down threadbare beige carpet and pulled out his Action Man figure from his hideaway base which was actually an old 'Hi-Tec' shoe box, between exposed chipboard wardrobe and his peeling bedroom wall. The Action Man was the latest model with moving eyes and a short spiky crew-cut, green camouflage and black M-16 assault rifle. The figure was his pride and joy because he still had the plastic case it came in. In fact, it was the only toy that he possessed. Action Man was a man that didn't take any kind of nonsense from anyone, someone that stood on his own two feet and dealt with any situation that arose. He knew how to speak to women; he knew how to deal with men. Action Man was fighting off the advancing smelly Hi-Tec trainer that doubled as an enemy tank. He threw himself onto the top of the trainer and was dragging the hurtling tank back with his brute strength.

"Aha, you thought that your tank could get through my Action Man power! You don't deserve to even battle me. I am the greatest of all time. I am…"

The boy's play was suddenly interrupted by a shout from the adjacent room.

"Toothy! Toothy get here now!"

The boy answered to 'Toothy' this was obviously not his birth name, just the name that he had been called since he could remember.

He instantly stood up and shot up to the room from where the call came.

"Yes, Mum?"

He entered his mother's bedroom and if he wasn't used to the overpowering smell of 'Charley' perfume it would have taken his breath away. The room was dimly lit by a solitary brown paisley pattern lamp that stood in the corner. The white tassels that at one time hung as pristine shiny white teeth were now all yellow and matted like a drunk's teeth smiling as he saw the pub about to open. A smouldering fire was lit in the fireplace, the heat it produced with its handful of coals was hardly keeping the room above chilly.

His mother stood with a black silky night dress that barely covered her modesty. She sat on the edge of her double bed that sank low with a combination of her weight and the used mattress that had lost its springiness with age. A larger woman with short dirty blonde hair and the occasional curl tucked under one of her chins. The top of her head was adorned with a limp black synthetic orchid. Her face was caked in make-up, which, to a casual observer, would have seemed odd on a rainy Tuesday afternoon but the boy was used to seeing his mother constantly made up.

"Come 'ere, Toothy, what have I told you about walking mud on the carpet?"

"Sorry, Mum, I was just trying to get out of my wet things quickly," replied the boy.

"Don't ever answer me back. Come here!"

The woman then slapped the boy with a left-handed backhand and sent him sprawling across the room and he fell in a heap like a sack of potatoes.

As he hit the floor, he began to cry and held the side of his face that now throbbed and was beetroot red from the blow. The woman then lifted him up with one hand and slapped him again with her left hand. She dropped him down again and snatched his Action Man from his grasp.

"No, give it back to me!" Toothy shouted.

"Now, you're telling me what to do!" shouted his mother.

"No, Mum, I wasn't... I mean... I just—" the boy stumbled over his words from his rising dread.

He then watched in horror as his mother held the Action Man stiff in her right hand and proceeded to pull off his head and threw it into the open fire, followed by both arms, both legs and then the torso. Toothy couldn't stand the sight of his plastic figure slowly melting and morphing into a gooey mess that coated the glowing coals. A distant lightning strike flashed, shortly followed by a rumble of thunder as he scampered like a scolded dog to his bedroom, jumped onto his unmade bed and cried into his pillow. Squashing the pillow into his face which made his breathing even more laboured as the claustrophobia of the pillow muted his bawling.

Eventually, he loosened his grip and closed his eyes but continued to see his mother's left hand slapping his face, but that did not hurt him the most; it was her hand yanking off the body parts. It was her left hand that had hurt him inside and out, always her left hand, always that hand. He could still see it when he closed his eyes and couldn't stop seeing it until he eventually fell asleep holding his pillow with tears tracking down both cheeks.

Year 1984

Part One: The Beast of Crompton Moor

Chapter 1
Albert and Dorothy Bradley

A silver-grey tawny owl glided gracefully back to the safety of her nest, clutching a twitching field mouse just as a stiff northern wind blew across the great expanse of Crompton Moor. It was an area of over 160 hilly acres of open barren undulating moorlands and ancient woods of dusty browns and vibrant greens. It was indeed a hidden gem adjacent to the town of Shaw and Crompton, which in turn lay on the outskirts of Greater Manchester in Northern Oldham, in the sleepy foothills of the South Pennines.

Deep in the undergrowth of Crompton Moor a startled red grouse flew out of the high wild grass and purple heather as Ken Goodwin started on his rounds. He parked up his motorised bicycle in the deserted gravel car park and began his long walk around the roughed moorlands. He enjoyed the daily routine and his long walk as he always did his best to keep himself active ever since leaving the Royal British Navy where he reached the most respectable rank of Lieutenant General.

Ken had kissed his wife Charlotte and set off at the crack of dawn, because he was the ranger at Crompton Moor Country Park and had been in love with the wildlife and the freedom of the open air for all of his life. That particular afternoon he was feeling fit as a fiddle as he got dressed. He put on his dark green waterproof jacket, trousers and his well-worn black walking-boots. He always carried his binoculars and his large telescopic camera with a dark green fisher man's hat on top of his dark red hair and sunglasses which completed his outfit. That spring day, he walked his usual path inspecting the recently constructed stonewall and the barbed wire fence that kept the neighbour farmer's sheep penned in. He also checked on the pack of roe deer that grazed on the moorland and ensured that all dogs were kept on leads near to the breeding pheasants.

Ken was more than glad to be back out and about since his vicious assault last month. He doesn't recall much about the attack, except that he was patrolling the woods late one evening last month and was spooked to hear an animal howl that he had not heard before. The next thing something broke through the tree line behind him and in the process of spinning around he lost his footing and slipped. The slip may have actually saved his life because whatever sprung at him only caught him with a glancing blow. The back of his neck was deeply scratched with some type of claw. The weight of the unknown creature had knocked into his shoulder and sent him rolling down into the purple heather and left him completely unconscious. Two days later he woke up in The Royal Oldham Hospital with scratch marks still on his shoulder. His other wounds had healed completely before he left hospital two weeks later. No one knew how he got to the hospital. He was found outside the main entrance unconscious, battered and bruised, because he didn't have any recognition of whatever attacked him so was unable to elaborate on anything to the police, hospital staff, or his frantic wife Charlotte.

Just as Ken was finishing off his walk around the darkening woods and had checked on the nesting birds when the moon slowly rose in the early evening sky. Suddenly without warning, a sharp pain exploded from his intestine, causing him to call out and bend over double. His call for help went unheard as there wasn't anyone within earshot to hear his painful cries. As he crouched down in the frozen, worn-out, brown muddy path he began to change. His hands tore and ripped as they elongated in front of his face. All of his bones, sinew, ligaments, muscle and tissue all rip and stretched. His once calloused working man's hands had now transformed into a gigantic throbbing claw covered in thick dark red hair. His jacket and trousers simultaneously split and fell to the muddy ground as his form almost doubled in size with muscular hairy arms and legs popping out. His face contorted and stretched into a wolf's muzzle with razor sharp fangs. As the fangs protrude from his mouth, the teeth were already coated with thick dripping saliva. The beast craved, it hungered for a taste; a taste for blood.

The werewolf stood where Ken had fallen. A huge figure standing over 8 feet tall, covered in thick red fur, billowing in the stiff evening breeze. The fur was not thick enough to completely cover his muscular physique beneath, which gently pulsed ready for action. His eyes were illuminated emeralds that blazed in the darkness. Now he could see everything around him. Hear the accelerated heartbeat of a panicked hare that scampered. The gloomy obscured woods were suddenly lit up into a bright ultra-high definitional world. Every groove in every tree became like a horizontal Grand Canyon in minute detail. His nose was filled with a million and one different scents floating in the spring-time air. Two miles deeper in the woods a female tawny owl picked the flesh off a field mouse for her hungry chirping owlets. Three miles away from the woods, the smell of the faraway fumes from the traffic and smoke in town filled his left nostril. Then through all the myriad of sounds and the cacophony of noise the werewolf heard the one sound that it prized above all others; a human heart beat. In fact, he heard two human hearts beats. The beast let out an ear-piercing howl at the full moon and then with one giant leap it was off to meet its prey.

A carrion crow squawked and rustled in the tall pine tree. The woods were silent except for this occasional bird call, but even that stopped when it sensed a presence walking far below under the thick canopy of leaves. The figure which now stalked through the undergrowth and every other animal could sense they were in the midst of the apex predator; the werewolf. A beast that didn't think, didn't feel, didn't reason, and just acted on instinct, an instinct to hunt, to kill, to feed.

In the open expanse of moorland, two figures trudge through the well-worn path and rapidly mudding grass verge. Both figures held a walking pole to support their slightly hunching gait as a result of the weighty green rucksacks on their backs. Albert and Dorie Bradley stopped to consult their brand-new walking map of 'Crompton Moor and surrounding walks'. This octogenarian couple had been married for more than forty five years. They first met in 1911 when Albert was on leave from the Royal Engineers and was visiting a friend when he met the nineteen-year-old Dorothy Harris on the dance floor at the King George V Coronation Ball. Albert knew from the first moment that he asked her to dance the jitterbug hop he was smitten. Maybe it was the ease that he led her across the dance floor, the way he spun her around and laughed as she lost her balance and collapsed into his grateful arms, but it was probably the way he completely lost himself in her eyes, a feeling that she could still bewitch him with today.

They were grandparents, indeed great grandparents but they never lost their teenage feelings for each other and had never spent a night apart. They had been walking for all of their lives but were new to rambling over the vast barren moors over Crompton.

"Is it left at the radio mast, Bert? The map says it's called Crow Knowl," asked Dorie.

"No, love, straight on I think," replied Albert.

"I'm sure we have been this way already, it's getting dark now, love, shall we just go back the way we came?" said Dorie.

"I'm not sure if that might be a longer route," said Albert.

A distant howl froze the two walkers; their exposure on the vast moors exaggerated their vulnerable position. The fear of not knowing which way to go started as a mild irritation but quickly became a blind panic. As the glow from the moon illuminated the edge of the woods, they could see a large figure emerging from the wood line. It walked upright, slightly hunched with huge broad shoulders and emerald eyes that shone against the silhouette of its face. It gave off a low but menacing growl that was like a well-tuned Harley Davidson revving up.

"Come on, love, let's head towards that light on the hill, I think it's a farm. Let's just keep on moving," said Albert.

"Bert, my legs are shaking I can't walk anymore." Dorie held Bert close and looked him straight in the eye. "Please, love, you go on, save yourself, save yourself," pleaded Dorie.

Bert just stared at Dorie's face and just let the tears flow as he whispered, "I love you, Doe."

Even though they saw the beast approaching when the attack did happen, it came suddenly and was brutal. The creature ambled towards the couple until he was twenty metres away and all of a sudden sprang through the air. Claws outstretched as Albert and Dorie clung together, the beast ripped them in half. They had died as they had lived, in each other's arms looking to each other for comfort.

Chapter 2
One Heather Hill

Inspector Clayton Rudd twisted the grey grooved dial, to turn up the volume of his brown brand-new Hitachi television. Gingerly, he sat down on his cream living room sofa which still had the faintest whiff of leather whenever sat upon. He gently placed his red steaming bowl of 'Quaker Oats' porridge topped with glistening oozing honey on the vintage dark red rosewood coffee table. With a sip of his milky coffee he settled down to watch 'TV-am Good Morning Britain'. The slightly annoying Roland Rat was doing his usual "Yeah, I'm a superstar" and cracking jokes with Kevin the Gerbil and his long-suffering minion Nick Owen. Clayton smiled at the thought of the only known case of a rat boarding a sinking ship that was TV-AM. The program had been struggling in the ratings recently until the introduction of Roland and stopped it sinking without a trace. The appeal of the annoying rat was somewhat lost on him, but sometimes in the morning, low brow entertainment is all that is required until the brain has woken up.

It was going to take a lot to wake him up today because he had just finished working a set of nights and always struggled to wake up for his first day shift. It was fair to say that he was more of a night owl than an early bird. So, he really needed his morning coffee and upcoming power shower to bring him to life.

To look at Clayton most people would not think that he was a mid-ranking police officer in the Manchester Constabulary.

Indeed, he was one of the youngest ever men to reach the position of inspector at the tender age of thirty two after several years of walking the beat and a brief stint as a police trainer. Maybe he could have gone even further, like his ex-wife, Hannah, who was currently acting chief inspector. Hannah and he had only dated for a short time when they had a child together, Jessica Rudd, who was just six years old. She spent the majority of time living with her mother and her soon-to-be new step-dad, the much younger, at twenty-five, Police Constable Michael Baker. To say it grated on him was an understatement, but he was just relieved that Jessica had his surname. To be honest, though, Hannah was pretty good when it came to visitation rights and letting her stay over. When Jess wasn't staying over, Clayton lived on his own.

Although he lived on his own, he was not lonely, he enjoyed his own company. Here, there was no one to tell him not to sit just in boxer shorts and there was no one there to tell him to stop using tooth pick at the dining table anymore. He had been living on his own since his break up with Hannah and despite popular belief, he didn't descend into a single life hovel but maintained his pride for his appearance and was exceptionally house-proud.

The fact that his ex-wife was promoted over him didn't bother him when they were briefly together. He always believed that if you worked hard, you would soon rise up the success ladder. He had taken advantage of his modest education and studied hard to emulate his biggest role model in life, his Uncle Patrick. His uncle had said that he would pay for a private education when he was only eight years old, but Clayton had told his parents that he had wanted to stay in Shaw, the town where all his friends lived.

Yes, he was a Shaw man born and bred; he was thick set and clearly looked after himself. Although not a fanatic gym member, he still managed to keep a trim figure and definitely postpone any middle-age spread with his healthy high protein diet and love for long-distance running. He was a man that took pride in his appearance, but his sense of style was not to everyone's taste as he currently sat in multicoloured super hero dressing gown, so he did not consider himself vain with his short cropped black hair and his piercing blue eyes set against his ever so slightly tanned skin from his mother's Anglo-Indian roots. As he sat at his coffee table, he brushed away a stray black lock that had fallen in front of his eye and rubbed his prickly chin which was covered in a couple days of stubble which you could sometimes get away with on the night shift but he knew that a wet shave was overdue.

The thick, sweet-smelling porridge crunched slightly as he glanced at the headline in 'The Sun' newspaper: 'Girl 11, taken in broad daylight'. His head shook slightly. This type of headline was becoming all too common. He again contemplated the possible link with his own current missing girl's case. A young girl, Elizabeth Brook from Failsworth, was abducted near a fun fair on the outskirts of Greater Manchester. He had already contacted the North Yorkshire Constabulary to compare notes because of the very high possibility of it being the same offender; a black van was seen leaving the scene by CCTV.

After he finished reading the article and his breakfast, he polished the last dregs of his newly acquired Columbian percolated coffee, turned off the TV and washed up his coffee cup and white and red 'Kellogg's' cereal bowl and then went upstairs for a power shower. Clayton liked to have all the latest modern convenience at home; he had for years a Walkman, VHS recorder and the new Commodore 64. His house was like a mansion for one person. He wandered into one of his three spare bedrooms to pick up a fresh towel. Between a moment of being

24

asleep and fully awake when you're on autopilot, he found himself staring at some mahogany photo frames on his light blue paisley wallpaper. The first photo was of him smiling, wearing a cap and gown, holding a scroll tied in a pink ribbon; the other one was him as a child on his fifth birthday, sitting on Uncle Patrick's shoulders.

Clayton had inherited the house from his uncle when he passed away six years ago. Actually, he had only lived in the house for the previous two years since he split up with Hannah. The smell of wood varnish still filled the living room when Clayton had first entered the house at the age of ten, when it was newly constructed.

Uncle Patrick had been an eccentric man who didn't have a family of his own. His life was dedicated to his career as an architect and a designer who worked on a number of contrasting buildings; the stunning Roman Catholic Metropolitan Cathedral in Liverpool and Forton Service Station on the M6 in Lancashire amongst others, but perhaps his uncle's most impressive accomplishment was the house that Clayton currently resided in.

One Heather Hill was a marvel of engineering, for it held a secret that was unknown to the outside world. Judging by the exterior it was a large detached five-bedroom house with spacious living rooms, grey brick work in keeping with the rural location, with a low stonewall that surrounded the front of the property. Standing in front of the house was a white porch at top of three stone steps straddled by two symmetrical hanging baskets of purple lavender stalks and cascading foliage. The light aroma of lavender scented the front garden and attracted the occasional passing bumble bee or a Peacock butterfly. The house stood isolated in its own grounds when it was first built but over the years five more terrace houses were added creating a small street in the middle of the rural fields and farmland.

Patrick had been one of the world's true one offs; he had the mind of genius and also the funds to realise his wishes. Since growing up in a post-World War II society so he had always had a distinct fear of the emerging Soviet Union as one of the Superpowers. The Reds as he used to call them. He believed, as a number of people did, that a nuclear strike against the West was more a matter of when than if.

Regardless of the political climate, Patrick was adamant that he was not going to be one of life's victims, he was going to be proactive. So, he designed his house with a very special extra feature. Clayton could clearly remember the smile on his uncle's face and how excited he was when showing him around for the first time.

"Clayton, as you may be aware that I don't consider myself the same as everyone else, I don't want to live in a boring two up two down house. Sometimes in life, you need a bit of magic, mystery and wonder. So why not have a house that has its own secret chamber, indeed its own Nuclear Bunker. Come and have a look, Clay, and see what is so special about my home with a difference."

Against the living room wall stood a large bookcase full of the classics from *The French Lieutenant's Woman* to *The Hound of the Baskervilles* but if you should choose to read *The Strange Case of Dr Jekyll and Mr Hyde* then the whole bookcase will open just like a door revealing a hidden staircase. His Uncle Patrick pulled the book and the lights illuminated the concrete staircase that went straight down to a land of the unknown. At the bottom of the stairs was a room about 3 metres across by 6 metres. It was a room that only had a few features: a large halogen strip light and on a coffee table was a large TV monitor that showed a live feed of the second room.

Clayton could clearly remember the conversation he had with his uncle.

"Why have you got a screen showing what is happening in the secure room?"

"It does look a little strange, Clay, but there is a perfectly simple explanation. My old university pal the now professor Rizwan is writing a paper called 'The Art of Mastering Complete Solitude' and he is going to observe me for a week and in return will give me coaching on how to keep a positive mental attitude while I'm alone," said Patrick.

"Gordon Bennett, uncle! You sure do cover all bases."

To the left of the screen was a tunnel, which after twenty metres led to an exit on the side of the hillside, the exit was covered by a tangle of prickly holly bushes, red poppies and wild roses which sprouted crimson flowers over the interlocking thorny vines.

The item that commanded the room was a huge metallic vault door that looked like it was taken straight out of a city bank. It was pure titanium and at least three feet wide with seven steel cylinders protruding off the edge. On the wall next to the vault door around shoulder height was a large red button that pressed once would open the immense door automatically. Look Clay, uncle used to say that door will keep anything out, a nuclear blast, a raging lion or even your mother on a good day.

Once inside the deafly quiet room there was a separate cubicle containing a duck egg blue toilet bowl and shower, a shiny black kitchen unit adorned with various aluminium kitchenalia from a spatula, colander and tin opener or two. For about two metres around the kitchen area there was black and white lino and the rest of the floor was bare concrete. Apparently, the kitchen area was the only place where spills needed to be cleaned up easily. Adjacent to the kitchen was a single bed already made with a light blue quilt and dark blue pillow propped on top. A grey free-standing treadmill stood idly at the foot of the bed. The rest of the space surrounding the bed was filled with row upon row of beans of every kind; kidney beans, baked beans, chili beans, mixed beans, beans with pork sausages and curried beans. Uncle Patrick's philosophy was that beans contained all the nutrients and vitamins a body needed to support itself. With all those beans, it was a good job that Uncle Patrick lived alone. When the mountain of beans eventually ceased, it was replaced by bags of soil stacked up against the wall and various troughs of different sizes and a large pond-shaped mould filled with soil on the floor underneath the biggest heat lamp that you ever saw in your life. "I know what you're thinking, Clay, but if I can't get any natural sunlight, I still need to grow my own vegetables." Then he said, "Up here for thinking, down there for dancing!" And then he systematically pointed to his head and feet to illustrate his point.

On the other side of the room was a bookshelf with a number of paperback books from 'How to Survive a Zombie Holocaust', which included some tips on how best to barricade your door, which household items are best for protection should you be surrounded. Another was '101 Ways to Save and Use Less water' which included a practical guide on how to consume one's urine and 'A thousand and One Origami Designs' if you fancied making better use of the pages in those books.

Clayton remembered thinking that he should have just stashed a bundle of back issues of the Beano. It's a shame he couldn't put an Atari console down there, that would be at least a few years well spent. He could master 'Demon Driver!' or learn how to outrun those pesky ghosts in 'Pac-Man'.

He had decided not to change the room in all the years since his uncle passed away and indeed had only been down a few times since acquiring the house. It felt as if he kept it the same then a little bit of his uncle would always remain down there, a bit of a shrine to one of life original one offs.

After Clayton's mother and Uncle Patrick's sister Joan passed away and not having any family of his own, the house, and indeed, his whole estate, passed on to him. It is what he wanted because, as he used to say, "Clay, you're my favourite nephew."

"That's because I'm your only nephew." It was always Clayton's coordinal response.

He was abruptly roused from his reminiscing by the high pitch telephone ring in his living room. Quickly, he tied the chords to his dressing gown and slipped the large fluffy peach towel under his arm and descended the stairs to answer it. The voice at the other end was his long-time police partner, DI Griffin Dunne, and Clayton could tell by his voice that it wasn't good news.

"Hi, Clayton, it's Griff, we have just been alerted that another girl has gone missing, she was last seen in Shaw.

Chapter 3
The Simpson Brothers

Leroy Simpson pushed the cream-coloured cassette tape into his car player and waited as the sound of the tape rotating turned into the damping off beat guitar, drums and smooth vocals of the legend Bob Marley 'stir it up, little darling stir it up'. The red Capri's speakers hummed as the bass kicked in and in unison the three men in car bobbed their heads to the rhythm. Leroy changed down gears as the car screeched up the road past the abundance of abandoned skeletal mills a reminder of the Shaw's once great past, which now seemed a long time ago. This post-industrial town had served him well over the years; he knew the surrounding country lanes were quiet enough to disappear from pursuers and remote enough to get a good head start.

Leroy wound down his driver window and flicked out his smoking cigarette butt with his large dark-skinned fingers on his multi ring adorned shovel like hands. Every kind of jewel was present on his ring; sapphires, rubies and a large gold sovereign ring with a diamond encrusted 'L'. His knuckles bore scars both old and new when he let his fists do the talking. Some punches for rival gang members that wandered on to his turf, a security guard or two that didn't hand over the readies and any of his bitches that gave him any shit.

"Yo, Frank, are you sure that today is collection day?" asked Leroy to Frank who was sitting in the front passenger seat.

"Yeah, man, my guy in Barclays says today is the day, but

we got to wait it out 'cause it could be anytime," replied Frank.

"Okay, let's just get there and wait for the van to show our kid. You better get down keep out of view, three black guys waiting in a car is going to look well sus," said Leroy

"All right, man," said Billy as he crouched down on the backseat along with his pump action shotgun.

The high street in the town centre was busy that Friday afternoon in early summer. Crowds were scattered across the pavement looking for bargains in what seemed like a multitude of charity shops a Woolworths and a Rumbelows. Cars and buses flooded the high street pumping out exhaust fumes which tainted the delicate country air with a faint smell of engine grease. Overlapping the smell of the road was the sweet smell drifting from the local bakery, freshly baked apple pies, hot summer puddings and steaming cupcakes cooling on racks.

People spilled out onto the pavement drinking outside the local high street public house 'The Bluebell'. Voices were raised as tattooed men wore dirty white vest and luminous yellow jackets enjoyed a refreshing lunchtime pint in the sunshine.

The shiny red Capri continued to wait in its parked position on the side street. Its engine had for some time been idle as barely visible smoke escaped from it vibrating exhaust pipe. The occupants anxiously waited for the right time to act. The three black men were all waiting, all nervous. Although none of the men were currently smoking, the interior of the car had a strong pungent smell of cannabis. But there was nothing relaxing about their current situation. Their adrenaline had built up their energy levels so they were now like coiled springs waiting to be released or finely tuned racehorses chopping at the bit. All three wore black puffy bomber jackets zipped up tight to their chins. Their attire was totally inappropriate for that time of year when the weather dictated that shorts and t-shirts were the order of the day.

After a minute or two of silence, Leroy pushed the driver's seat all the way back to give himself maximum legroom and pulled on his black gloves, he then turned to talk to the Billy crouching down on the back seat who was biting on his index finger.

"Billy, for God's sake keep your pump down!"

Billy crouched in the foetal position making sure his head and his pump action shot gun stayed under the height of the window. A strange mixture of fear and excitement coursed through his body. This is what he had dreamed about for nearly eight years now. Being part of the gang for real meant that he was in the action not just a bystander. Of course, he had always been affiliated with the Simpson boys being the youngest brother of the three. His previous role had been peddling cannabis to the local pot heads like Cock-Eyed Colin and his old school mates but now he had served his time and now he was in the big leagues: an armed robber. He stretched out on the seat nodded and swallowed as a bead of sweat formed on his forehead and dripped down his nose.

"Yeah, and don't do a ting, we haven't planned for, just because it's your first job don't be gung-ho, hot heads get people killed," said Frank who was shifting uncomfortably in the front passenger seat.

Leroy swivelled in his seat and spoke to both of his brothers while pulling his pump action shotgun from between the driver's seat and the door

"Don't worry, Frank, we all know our roles. Billy, you're in charge of getting the loot, I'll deal with any would-be Charlie Bronsons who have a fucking death wish."

A woman with a sharp bottled red fringe, heavily made up

eyes and dark lips, crossed the road holding a young boy's hand. She had to trot slightly to avoid a white Group4 van which slowed and parked half on the road, half on the pavement. A large muscular man wearing a black helmet with the visor down and a white shirt with a red Group4 insignia on his pocket jumped out of the back of the van. He walked briskly into the bank and came out a few moments later with money in a grey suitcase. At that same precise moment, the shiny red Capri car came speeding around the corner and the three men jumped out with their black balaclavas down and their pump-action 12-bore shotguns up. With a shotgun pointing directly in the Group4 security guard's face, Leroy shouted out his instructions.

"Get your arse on the ground and don't move a fucking muscle."

The quivering security guard dropped to the pavement outside the bank and lay on the ground in the spread-eagle position. Still, he had hold of the grey money suitcase as Billy grabbed it out of the prone man's grasp. Instantly an injection of bright orange gas exploded into the air with a high pitch squeal. It stained Billy's black bomber jacket and discoloured his face. Instantly his panic and frustration was taken out on the security guard who was still lying next to the erupting suitcase. He put his size 11 steel toe-capped boot right through the guard's head, sending his black helmet skipping down the road thumping into a green litter bin, toppling even more waste food into the already littered street. The second kick knocked the guard out as a squirt of blood and a couple of teeth escaped his unconscious mouth.

The three men knew that the major score was inside the van which could hold up to five money cases at any time. Frank and Leroy swiftly proceeded to use their pump action shotguns and whacked the side of the Group4 van, denting the white aluminium bodywork with every violent blow.

With no joy in gaining entry to the van Billy then took matters into his own hands and grabbed a small boy from the rapidly thinning crowd. He thrust the barrel of his shotgun into his stomach then his kidneys as the boy face creased in pain and anguish. The boy stood speechless probably from the pain of the shotgun and the life-threatening situation he found himself in. Billy screamed instructions to the unseen occupants of the security van.

"Open the fucking door, or I'll shoot the kid, open the door now, open the door now! I'm gonna blow this kid all over your van."

Billy then turned the boy round and screamed directly into his face.

"Tell them, kid, to open the door; you better start pleading for your life, start talking."

The boy just stood there frozen to the spot, unable to speak, his bottom lip quivered and his legs shook.

Leroy and Frank tried a different tact and shot at the driver and passenger windows. Although the windows splattered and cracked beyond belief, their integrity remained and denied access to the armed robbers. Billy continued to scream at the unseen occupants of the van as a well-built man wearing a grey three-piece suit approached him with his hands up.

"Please, please take me as your hostage, let the boy go, you're scaring him he's pissed his pants," said the man in the suit.

Billy's face contorted with disgust as his nostrils registered the pungent urine turning the boy's beige trousers clingy and dark. He looked down at the boy's wet patch down his leg and spat and cursed as he threw him back towards the cowering crowd. The boy immediately darted back to a distraught woman with red hair who was whaling like a Banshee. The boy and the lady hugged as the tears rolled down both of them, yet still the boy was silent. Instead of disappearing from the street, he held his position and refused to let the woman lead him away as he watched the unfolding scene.

Billy pointed his shotgun towards the suited man and shouted, "Get your arse here." Suddenly, he thrust the butt of his shotgun into the man's gut sending him doubling over onto the pavement. The man's air in his lungs whooshed out as the wind was knocked out of him. Billy teeth began to grind and the veins in his forehead throbbed under his balaclava as he stood over the now coughing and wheezing suited man with his shotgun lodged in the back of the man's head. Again, Billy shouted to the occupants of the Group4 van, "You have exactly five seconds to open the hatch or I'm going to blow this guy's brains out... One... two... three... four..."

Just before Billy could say the word five, his standing foot was whipped out from beneath him, causing him to crash onto the pavement with a thud and a crack of skull hitting concrete. For the merest fraction of a second, he lost control of the shotgun which gave the suited man an opportunity to attack. Both men grappled on the road with the barrel of the shotgun held fast between them as they rolled back and forth getting covered in dust and debris from the pavement and road. The scratching sound of the two men rotating on the ground was punctuated by the occasional sound of a squelch as they squashed discarded food by the overflowing rubbish bin. Eventually, both men used the other to lever themselves back to their feet while still managing to keep hold of the vertical shotgun. As the two men fought, a distant sound of police sirens could be heard coming closer. The Tactical Armed Response units were only a few minutes away.

Frank screamed frantic instructions to his young brother.

"Billy, for fuck's sake leave it, the FEDs are coming! We need to go now; we need to fucking go now!"

"I'll deal with this fucking tosser!" shouted Leroy.

Leroy strode towards the grappling couple and held his shot gun in the firing position and waited to offload on the suited man. Just waited one second, two seconds bang. He took a shot at the man in the suit. The man's left shoulder instantly exploded as the bullet cartridge ripped right through him with a searing burn and a cracking of bones. He collapsed and hit the pavement with a thud that almost knocked him out. As he fell his right hand clutched at the barrel of the shotgun trying to halt his falling. A finger caught on the trigger and the weight of his falling body pulled it back. The action fired a bullet straight through Billy's chin into his brain and out the top of his head followed by an assortment of brain, blood and bile. Billy's body hit the roadside and spasmed as his muscles worked out the last of their available energy in a bloody writhing mess.

Frank screamed as his younger brother's head exploded in an ear-piercing blast followed by a cloud of crimson. Leroy stood in shock for a number of seconds as bits of brain fell back down to earth. He blanked out the police sirens which continued to get closer by the second and his brother's voice screamed in his ear and tried to jolt him out of his daze.

"Let's go, Leroy, the fucking pigs are coming," shouted Frank.

"Wait, I'm going to blow away that have a go hero bastard!" shouted Leroy.

Frank sprinted the few yards and jumped into the still turning over shiny red Capri get-away car. The tyres screeched up the road and made its way away from the scene as the police sirens screeched ever closer. Being left there did not bother Leroy as he strode towards the bleeding suited man writhing in the bloodied street. He aimed the shotgun at the stricken man's chest. Several thoughts went through Leroy's head; he knew now that he wouldn't be getting away. As he saw Frank in the Capri disappeared down the road towards Rochdale. He knew that if he changed cars three times before taking off his balaclava, he wouldn't get caught. But he also knew that the man who had just pulled the trigger that killed Billy wouldn't be far behind him. He held his pump action shotgun in both hands and aimed methodically, making sure that the man's heart was in his sights. The next moment, the shotgun was discharged with a billow of smoke and jerk of the barrel.

Chapter 4
Jonathan Evans

Griffin Dunne sat in the passenger seat while Clayton Rudd, his partner of five years, parked his unmarked burgundy Jaguar XJ12 series police car in the car park to the rear of the row of shops behind Shaw High Street. They were following up on the last known eye witness to have seen the young girl Hazel Fry before she went missing just two days ago. The local press had already helped to circulate the girl's photograph and a description of her red-hair and freckled face had been sent to all of the North-West police forces.

A shiny red Capri car was idling on a side street waiting as the two detectives entered 'Bygone times' sweetshop and stood in the entrance as the radio played the last chorus of 'The Safety Dance'. They looked like the police version of 'Laurel & Hardy' with Clayton being tall with a slight muscular build and his partner Griffin who it was fair to say had never darkened the door to a gym in his fifty-five years of life. He was short and round with short, grey, side-parted hair. Although he was not quite morbidly obese, he definitely could be described as having a salad dodger's double chin, hidden slightly by his trim greying moustache and beard.

He used to be a lot fitter when he worked in the firearms department in the Greater Manchester Constabulary for all told twenty years. But for the last five he had worked with Clayton in CID in the serious crime division.

Griffin's tight-fitting shirt opened slightly between each button as he held out his ID badge to the Middle-aged lady behind the shop counter and said, "Hello, love, are you Cissie Barlow? We spoke earlier on the phone."

The woman had sharp angular features and greying streaks against her black hair, which was tied back with a pink ribbon. She leant slightly on the wooden counter that was full of blue and green sweet boxes and a weighing machine with an assortment of grey circular discs weights neatly piled up in order of size. Behind her was a vast assortment of glass jars filled with multi-coloured sweets, wiping her glasses on her pink apron she smiled and leant further across the counter to have a closer look at their IDs.

Griffin continued, "I am Detective Inspector Dunne and this is my colleague Inspector Rudd, may we have a word with you about the disappearance of Hazel Fry. I understand you saw her on the day she disappeared."

"How do you do, Detectives? Yes, Hazel came in a few days ago on Tuesday last week, I think," said Cissie. Her accent was not a local one for she had only lived in Shaw for seven years since leaving the Home Counties.

"So, you are able to make a positive identification, are you sure that it was Hazel?" asked Clayton.

"Yes, Inspector, I am positive that it was Hazel because you see she was one of my regular customers and would often pop in for her sherbet dip and a can of lilt," replied Cissie.

"Mrs Barlow, do you remember how Hazel was on the day she came in the shop, was she acting strangely?" asked Inspector Rudd.

"No, she was fine, very chatty and seemed in a good mood. She bought some sweets and then said that her mum had given her extra pocket money so she was going to treat herself," said Cissie.

"Did she say where she was going or mention what she planned to do for the rest of the day?" asked Griffin Dunne.

"She mentioned that she was buying a 'Cabana' chocolate bar for her mother. So, I assumed that she went home."

"Thank you, Mrs Barlow. Did you happen to notice which way she went after leaving the shop?" asked Clayton.

"I remember saying goodbye to her and asking her to say hello to her mum from me and she went left pass the Barclays Bank, I think," she said.

"Thank you, Mrs Barlow, you have been very helpful, and can I just ask did you notice any one hanging around or anyone acting suspiciously that day?" asked Griffin.

"Not really. It was quite a busy day that day in and out of the shop. You see, I was having the rear window panel fixed," said Cissie.

"Oh, I see. Who was fixing your window? There is a chance that they may have noticed something," asked Clayton.

"I'm not sure of his name, but I have his card here somewhere," she said.

Both police officers waited while Cissie rummaged underneath her cash till until she found a business card and handed it over to Clayton who read aloud it 'Barry Stone, Manchester-based handyman: no job too big or too small 0161 11151623'.

"Thank you, Mrs Barlow, for your time. We will be in touch if we need any more information, but for now please don't hesitate if you remember anything else, please ring me no matter how small you think it is," said Clayton.

Both men shook her hand and thanked her for her help. "Oh,

would you mind putting this poster in your window? The more people who see Hazel's face the more chance we have of jogging their memory," said Griffin as he handed over a rolled-up piece of paper. She unravelled it and could see a photo of Hazel Fry waving on the top of a slide below the words 'Missing' and an appeal for information. Cissie gasped and put her hand to her mouth as her eyes began to moisten.

"I'm sorry, gentlemen, it's just a shock to see her on a missing poster. Yes, of course, I will put it up. It is the least I can do," she said.

Both men gave a curtsey nod to Cissie and turned to leave the shop. As they were leaving, a tall woman with long bright red hair and a boy in beige pants and dark blue duffle coat walked in.

"Here you go, miss," said Clayton as he opened the door for the lady and the boy.

Griffin stopped in the doorway of the shop and turned to Clayton.

"While we're here, we might as well get something for the boys back at the station."

"Oh yes, the boys back at the station and your very own six-pack." Clayton tapped Griffin's belly and both men smiled. Griffin perused the shelves and picked up a large bag of Polo mints a pack of Opal fruits and a packet of milk chocolate Dazzles. He continued to scan the array of brightly coloured sweets to see if anything else caught his fancy. While Clayton waited for Griffin to satisfy his appetite, he noticed the interaction between the duffel coated boy and his red-haired mother. The boy pleadingly moved his right hand from his chin away six inches and back like a golf flag vibrating in a hurricane.

"Please, Mum, let's get this. It's my favourite one," signed the boy.

"Jonathan, it's just too expensive; I don't have that many pennies with me," signed back the woman.

"Oh, please, Mum, I won't ask for anything again," signed the boy.

Jonathan held onto the large bag of multi-coloured pear drops and put his thumb up.

"Those used to be my favourite too, young man," interjected Clayton.

The lady looked up at him a little surprised at the comment, she hadn't been aware that he was watching their conversation.

"Do you sign?" asked the woman.

"Just a little, my late father was deaf for the last few years of his life."

"Sorry, my name's Clayton."

"Hello, my name is Kristina and this is my son Jonathan."

Clayton shook Kristina's hand and then gave Jonathon a high five.

"Look, I'm getting my friend's sweets and I don't really want a pocket full of coppers and lose change, so please, you will be doing me a massive favour if you allow me buy your lad the bag of sweets," said Clayton.

Then Kristina smiled a shy smile and signed to her son "What do we say, Jonathan?"

"Thank you." The boy mouthed as he again touched his chin and moved his hand forwards then beamed a smile of pure joy.

"Thank you," said the woman, "that is very kind of you." She smiled at Clayton and her whole face lifted for the briefest of seconds and an attractive glint flashed across her eyes. He paid for the boy's sweets and also the assortment of goodies that Griffin piled onto the counter and left the sweetshop.

Kristina then signed, "We just need to pop to Video Cave

and drop off the 'The NeverEnding Story' before we go home."

Both detectives casually walked up the walkway which ran perpendicular to the high street towards where the car was parked when Griffin said, "Oh, I'll meet you back at the car. I need to pick up a card I mean err something."

Griff, suddenly, felt as if he had been caught bunking off from school.

"Don't worry, Griff, if you're getting a wedding card for Hannah. It's okay. It's about time that we both moved on and Michael seems like a good bloke I know that Jessica likes him," said Clayton putting on a brave face.

"Yes, I'm getting a card. Ruby and I have been invited; just to the evening do though," muttered Griffin.

"No worries, Griff, you get the card and I'll see you back at the car," said Clayton.

Clayton strolled to his burgundy Jaguar. Kristina's eyes and smile must have left quite an impression on him because for some reason a cheesy grin wouldn't leave his face.

Suddenly, there was an almighty crash and commotion at the far end of the high street as a throng of people began to run with anguished expressions amongst the screams or terror. Over these screams were the rasp voices of men shouting out various instructions. Clayton bolted to his car and drove it around the front, to main road where he could see three men waving pump action shotguns. A security guard was lying on the ground. Again, one of the men shouted, "Keep your arse on the ground and don't move a fucking muscle!"

One of the shotgun wielding men tried to grab the grey suitcase when it omitted bright orange smoke which contaminated the contents of the case and also polluted the air with pungent sulphur that choked the security guard and the armed man alike.

There is nothing like fear to make people act irrationally and this armed robber was not immune to acting on impulse. He booted the stricken security guard twice in the head, sending the helmet into the street and the second kick sent his teeth into the street. The unknown shotgun wielding robber then ran into the fleeing crowd and snatched Jonathan from the grasp of his mother. Kristina bawled into the balaclava face of the man, but he knocked her to the ground with butt of his 12-bore pump action shotgun. The masked man then without reason or justification crashed the butt of his shotgun into Jonathan's stomach and pressed it deep into his back.

The other two masked men were banging on the side of the Group4 van demanding that the hatch be opened so they could get their hands on more money that wasn't tainted orange but the Group4 van door remained secure as the masked man shouted, "Open the fucking door, or I'll shoot the kid, open the door now, open the door!"

The two other men then unloaded their shotguns into the van but without success as the windshield and windows held firm. Clayton knew that Jonathan's life was in terrible danger and a feeling overtook him, not self-preservation, but the opposite he put his own life in jeopardy to try to save Jonathan's life.

"Please, please take me as your hostage, let the boy go, you're hurting him; he's pissed his pants," shouted Clayton.

The masked man released his hold on Jonathan's blue duffle coat and the little boy disappeared into the cowering crowd. Clayton didn't see or expect the butt of the shotgun as it wrecked his insides. The sudden pain brought him to his knees. It bent him over gasping for breath with the wind knocked out of him. Putting himself in such a dangerous situation didn't seem the wisest thing he had ever done, but he knew he stood more of a chance than small, frightened Jonathan. Through the throbbing ache in his stomach which occupied most of his attention, he could still hear voices shouting around. One voice stood out the man standing over him counting.

A sixth sense told him that he needed to act now before it was too late. With all of his might, he swung his right arm and connected with the back of the man's left knee bringing the masked robber crashing to the ground. The shotgun went straight up in the air as the Clayton sprung onto him and struggled to gain the advantage. Like a sycamore seed spinning to earth, both men clutched the shotgun and span around and around. The dirt, grit and litter from the road embedded itself into Clayton's cheeks and forehead as he turned his 15-stone frame and crashed to the pavement wedging the masked man against it. Both Clayton and the masked man, whose balaclava was now scuffed and pulled so now only one eye could be seen through the woollen hole manage to incredibly pull their bodies upright both still holding fast to the vibrating shotgun. Both men knew that to lose this struggle could mean their freedom or their life.

When the blast came, it is true to say it came without a warning; the force of his shoulder exploding hardly allowed his brain to react at all and Clayton just collapsed. His hands instinctively grasped for support and caught the shotgun trigger on their way down. The explosion of the shotgun was the last sound Clayton heard before his body went into shock, writhing from pain then ultimately concussion. His body just could not cope with the stress of the situation from the bullet wound and the fall onto the solid tarmac of the road.

Wailing voices filled the air as one of the masked men ignored the approach of sirens and the wheel spin of the red Capri, as he strode towards the unconscious body of Clayton. As he walked, he cocked the shotgun ready for a fatal shot. The man's attention was so focused on avenging his gang mate's sudden death. So, he hadn't noticed the boy with soiled pants creeping up behind him. Jonathan had used all of his courage to ignore his complete dread so he could help the stricken man from the sweetshop. He crept up behind the masked man and suddenly with all of his strength, pain and anguish that he felt, kicked the shotgun-wielding masked man right smack between his legs in his meat and two veg. The man screamed and fell to the ground as the shotgun went off into the air, scattering a group of town pigeons off the top of Barclays Bank as the cartridge then harmlessly fell back down to earth in the adjacent car park.

Before the masked man could pick himself up off the ground, the boy had already disappeared down a walkway and out of sight. Through the ache in his groin, he gingerly got to his feet and cocked the shotgun again to finish off the bleeding Clayton. Before he could raise his shotgun, a rubber bullet came from behind him and knocked him down again.

"Keep looking at me," the voice shouted again and again. Four heavily armed policemen wearing protective vests approached in unison with their firearms pointed at the fallen suspect. Two other policemen went to assist the stricken men.

Griffin leant over Clayton, reassuring him that an ambulance was on its way

"Hold on, Clayton, please. For Christ's sake, Clayton, hold on!"

Chapter 5
Sabu and Dimple Chopra

A distant blue lightning bolt snapped like a cranky crocodile as the heavy rain pounded on the blue waterproof canopy of the two-man tent. Sabu and Dimple Chopra struggled to tie the last of the guy-ropes to the embedded camping peg, to stop the tiger claws of the wind from ripping out the poles. The deserted woodlands and moors of Crompton had seemed like a good idea at the time to get away from everything. But now, as the weather had changed and turned their romantic weekend break into a fight with tent poles and faces full of wind, mud and grass.

Dimple's mood hadn't improved that evening as she constantly reminded Sabu that it was his idea to go camping for the weekend. She was doing her best to hide the strength of her disappointment from him; she didn't want to completely ruin the already strained atmosphere any further. She had imagined that when he said about going away for the weekend he had meant a weekend sight-seeing up the Eiffel Tower in Paris, visiting Vatican City in Rome or at the very least a Spa weekend in Manchester for their fifth wedding anniversary. But oh no, getting back to nature is just what the doctor ordered!

"Bloody hell," cursed Dimple under her breath with a wince as the precipitation lashed her head with a mixture of rain and hail. Her long black hair with blond streaks was now flattened against her forehead and down the side of her rouge cheeks. I work twelve-hour night shifts in The Royal Oldham Accident &

Emergency paediatrics department to put up with this on my only weekend off in four. He knows that I don't like walking at the best of times and we come to the middle of bloody nowhere!

"All done, love, the ropes should hold back an elephant charge," Sabu announced as he crawled on all fours into the tent next to Dimple.

She rolled her eyes and let out a deep breath and turned over.

"I'm sorry, love. They said it would be fine this weekend. That bloody Michael Fish, I'll never believe him again," said Sabu as he leaned over to cuddle her.

"Well, at least we had dinner before the weather set in. So, we have time for whatever," he said.

She turned her body away from him and propped her head on her hand. "You might have got some if we'd gone to the Hilton!"

Dimple quickly turned back to him and said, "Listen when you said 'something naughty', I thought you meant a romantic weekend away, or at the very least a double dessert at Wetherspoons, not illegal camping in Crompton bloody Moor!"

"You always used to like the unexpected, quirky and exciting," said Sabu.

"Maybe ten years ago! Now my idea of excitement is a lie-in and breakfast in bed!" she said as she turned again in a huff.

Sabu shrugged his shoulders and let out a big sigh, turned back and sat up in the tent. He hadn't the heart to tell her the truth. They weren't really on a romantic weekend he was just lying low for a while. He had been selling secrets about his place of work to an organised gang; the best way to forge a cheque, how to fake a credit card and when was the best opportunity to rob a bank and get away before the police caught up with you. Of course, he had pangs of guilt about selling this information but Barclays Bank

48

didn't pay its bank clerks the best and too often he had been overlooked for the team leader position. The money obvious had come in useful paying for the surprise luxury five-star trip to Malta next month. But for right now this romantic trip was the best excuse to get away from home for a few days because that last bank job was a real disaster.

One of the gang members was killed at the scene, a Group4 security officer was still in a coma fighting for his life, a member of the public too was fighting for their life after a shotgun took half his shoulder off and one of the gang members was arrested at the scene. But what scared him the most was the thought of the other brother Frank, who was his secret contact, was on the run. He didn't fancy his chances if he popped over to take out his frustration on him. As a slight shiver went down his spine, he pulled out a white packet of cigarettes with a purple square from his coat pocket and put one in his mouth and turned back towards Dimple.

"Do you want a ciggie?"

"Might as well," grudgingly responded Dimple.

"Oh, you're in the mood for a smoke at least!" huffed Sabu.

"Ha ha, funny!" she said with an exaggerated cheesy grin.

Sabu took out another 'Silk Cut' cigarette from the packet and handed one to her. He leaned over to light up her cigarette when they both froze as a guttural howl came from across the woods.

"What the fuck was that Sabu!" shouted Dimple.

"I haven't got a bloody clue, it's probably just some kids prating about," responded Sabu.

"I don't think so, it sounded so real and close and besides who is gonna prat about in this weather?"

There was another howl but this time a lot louder and not so far in the distance. Whatever was there, there was no doubt that it was getting closer with each passing moment.

"What the hell is out there?" said Dimple in urgent whisper.

"I don't know, probably an injured fox or something. I'm going to take a look," he said.

"No, Sabu, don't go out there! Don't leave me here alone! Stay here maybe it will just go away," pleaded Dimple.

"I'll just take a look; I'll only be a minute or two. It may just scarper when it sees the light from the torch," he reassured.

"Okay, but just be careful and what if it isn't an injured fox then what?" she asked.

"Don't worry, I've got my Swiss army pen knife in my pocket and a quick jab on the nose will send any animal packing," Sabu responded.

She attempted a half reassuring smile but the smile didn't reach her eyes. As Sabu cautiously unzipped the tent and picked up his torch. Slowly he stepped out into the raging wind and rain and then closed the zip from the outside. Dimple listened intently as she heard his heavy walking boots squelch in the rapidly forming mud outside. All was quiet apart from the sound of the rain battering the tent. Then she heard the sound of gasping for breath followed by a choking noise which echoed through the darkness and pierced her heart and hopes. She brought her knees in close and tucked them under her chin then wrapped her arms around her legs. Although she didn't realise, she began to rock slowly forward and back as she listened intently for any sound coming from outside. *Was the choking sound made by Sabu? Could it be a mating call of the Great British Badger?* she heard they can be really loud at this time of year.

The next second something crashed through the trees and landed with a loud thud. Dimple let out a shriek with the sudden crash close by. Then silence. Even the heavy rain seemed to cease and hold its breath, unwilling to make a sound. She crept to the zip to take a look out of the tent. Tentatively she reached out towards the zipped entrance and called out barely over a whisper Sabu... Sabu... Sabu?

Sabu's name stuck in her throat as a giant claw ripped through the side of the canvas and lifted the tent poles clean into the air, where the wind caught the limp canopy and it flew off into the moonlit night sky. Dimple was now exposed on all fours looking up at a gigantic beast standing at eight feet tall above her, peering down with razor teeth illuminated against its red muzzle. Its muscles flexed under his coarse red hair that was soaked against its steaming body. Piercing emerald eyes full of primeval rage shone from the head of the werewolf. Dimple whimpered and begged pleas fell on deaf ears. "No, no, please no..."

The werewolf struct with rage and precision with one swift swipe from its powerful claw and it tore the helpless woman in two.

Chapter 6
Charlotte Goodwin

Ken Goodwin paced up and down his red flowery corridor carpet. Three to five days delivery, so it must come today it was the fifth day. Charlotte would be back soon from the bakery in town, a postal delivery now when she was out would save numerous awkward questions. Then around the curved street came the welcome sight. Oh yes, yes Ken could see a bright red jacket making its way down his road. Joe McClusky was on his delivery rounds. Come on Joe, come on. Ken's frustration grew as Joe meandered his way down the street. He seemed to pop to every house before getting to his front door. Ken opened his front door and waited on the door step for Joe to reach him like a little boy bursting for the toilet, he hopped from foot to foot.

"Oh, hello, Ken, how are you doing?" asked Joe.

"Good, thanks, Joe, mustn't grumble," replied Ken.

"Well, it's a good job you're in. I've got a parcel for you."

"A parcel, that's a nice surprise," said Ken.

Joe handed over the small brown parcel and then went rummaging in red Royal Mail bag for his clipboard and pen.

"The flipping clipboard, I spend half my life searching for the thing. Maybe one day things will be electronic. Hey, Ken."

"We live in hope, Joe."

"Oh, here it is, could you print your name and sign next to it." said Joe.

Ken did his best to keep his frustration in check while Joe

rambled on.

"Are you doing some catalogue shopping? My eldest Joanne, has recently got into jogging. Everyday something is coming in the post for her sweatbands, wristbands, trainers you name it. Tried to get me into it but I do enough bloody walking I told her. Look at me chatting away I could talk the hind leg off a donkey my wife says."

Ken signed for the parcel and wished Joe a good day. Joe was barely out of the front garden when Charlotte came around the corner laden with two bulging plastic shopping bags. He quickly opened up the little rubbish bin storage unit and placed the small brown parcel on top of one of the waiting black bags, then trotted up the road to relieve his wife from her heavy load.

"Looks like you've bought half the shop, love," said Ken.

"Well, we needed teas for the next few days and we were out of milk and bread," replied Charlotte.

She let out an audible sigh of relief as Ken grabbed the two bags which was a good job because the plastic handle had started to cut into her hand leaving red lines across her palms.

"Do we have any post?" asked Charlotte.

"No, nothing today, I was just saying hello to Joe."

"That's you all over Ken, a friend to everyone."

Ken heart sank a little when he noticed that the small door of the bin hut was left slightly ajar but good job Charlotte didn't notice. She was more preoccupied in kicking off her shoes and having a nice cup of tea and a chocolate digestive.

It was not until Charlotte's evening bath that Ken had the opportunity to retrieve the stashed parcel. He picked it up half covered with moisture because it had sunk down into half-filled bin bag and took it straight to the work-shop in the back garden. There, he placed the parcel onto his dusty wooden work bench next to his worn blue metallic vice and tore off the brown parcel paper. Inside a thin layer of protective bubble wrap was a shiny industrial strength reinforced pair of iron handcuffs.

The next evening, as Ken and Charlotte were just finishing off the last of their homemade sherry trifle, Ken had a feeling that what he was about to say would not go down very well with Charlotte.

"I might need to pop out later to do an evening round, love," said Ken.

"Oh, do you have to, love, I don't think it very safe anymore since those killings last month," said Charlotte.

"I know, love, it was awful but that is all the more reason to make sure that everyone is out before dark," said Ken.

"Just be careful, love. I can't believe that you were on Crompton Moor the day of those horrendous murders. It's just a good job you went up to the Fitzmaurice Farm," said Charlotte with a quizzical glance.

Ken smiled a nervous smile as he thought he really needed to change the subject as he poured another strong cup of black tea from the lukewarm yellow porcelain teapot. A month ago, when the police came around to interview him, he had pleaded with Charlotte to give him an alibi just until he could figure things out. Charlotte had indeed given him an alibi for the night in question. It was the night of their weekly heads up poker challenge; she had taken all his chips with a straight flush on the river beating his full house. *Why she had given Ken an alibi without questioning his true whereabouts was something that was hard to justify to herself.* Maybe deep down she knew that her husband wouldn't hurt a fly, she didn't know if she was doing the right thing but with all her being, she tried to keep her family together sometimes it is a real struggle to turn a blind eye.

"I'm sorry to nag, love. It just sends a shiver down my spine when I think of you there all by yourself," said Charlotte.

"I'll just take the scooter for a quick check tonight. But don't wait up, love, I might pop over to Martin's for a quick cheeky dram," said Ken.

"Oh yes, there's nothing quick about your quick drinks with Martin," teased Charlotte.

Ken chuckled and stood up to clear the table of the two ornate leaves glass bowls with the sticky red remains of the jelly and cream. As he went to pick up Charlottes jelly smeared bowl, she grabbed his hand and said, "You would tell me, love, if anything was wrong? I'm still not sure why you asked me to tell the police that you spent the whole of that night with me last month. It's only because I know you that I trust you, love."

"I know, Lottie, love."

Ken's bottom lip quivered ever so slightly as he took the bowls to the kitchen sink.

Chapter 7
Ken Goodwin

The rising August moon glowed orange as it glided slowly in the late evening sky. Far below, Ken trudged his way deeper into Crompton Moor woods. He passed a carpet of purple heather which covered the moors and the newly planted ash trees which grew in conjunction with the long-established grand beech. He zigzagged through the long-shaded pines until he found the thick sturdy oak trees. Eventually, he found the most mature tree with well-established roots and trunk and should be immovable. He stood right up to the tree and could barely put his arms around its great trunk. With great difficulty, he stretched and fastened his brand-new pair of iron handcuffs. He only had just enough reach left to place the handcuff key into his top shirt pocket. Ken clicked both hand shackles closed tight and slid down the course tree trunk and scratched his right cheek slightly against the rough bark. At the base of the tree, he sat down on a protruding root along with the yellow buttercups and red poppies. Slowly, his eyes filled up with moisture until he could no longer keep the tears for rolling down his cheek. His whole body shook as he sobbed like a child.

He had long since fallen asleep and only woke when the change came over him. Instantly, he shot up and thrashed against the tree, trying to break free so violently that bits of bark began to splinter and fly off. As the steel chain scraped against the trunk, it exposed the light wood underneath the dark outer core.

As a man, he did not have a chance of breaking out of the steel handcuffs but that soon altered. The moon was now in its apex and it reappeared in front of a passing heavily laden grey cumulonimbus cloud about to drop its load. Eventually, Ken ceased his violent thrashing and began to transform. His hands slowly elongated, twisted and sprouted coarse dark red hair. They doubled in size and burst open the tight-fitting handcuffs. His knees instantaneously cracked and were pushed in on themselves, so now his leg bent forwards instead of backwards. Two giant hairy clawed feet popped out of Ken's walking boots. His new Park Ranger white shirt bulged as he grew in size. Nearly all of Ken's clothing burst at the seams and fell to the ground, the only part of material that hung to the gigantic beast was his loose-fitting elastic waterproof pants that clung to his now muscular thighs and now resembled beach shorts that ended at werewolf's knees.

After only a few moments, Ken had completely disappeared and now there stood a muscular, savage beast that instantly flung the handcuffs deep into wood with disdain and then ripped through the great oak with a double swipe of his great claws. That was the tree's punishment for even daring to try and chain the werewolf. With a thud the tree crashed to the ground in a hail of branches, leaves and a fleeing red squirrel. The newly freed beast raised his claws in the air and howled in triumph sending any remaining wildlife in close proximity running for cover. Various smells were inhaled; the rain that had just started to pour over everything in sight, reminiscent of a tropical monsoon. The sound of a multitude of animals filled the werewolf senses and once more one stood out as the most prized; the sound of a human heart. And again, the sound of two human's hearts beating was double the prize. He could see with his enhanced vision through the rain and mist a sky blue a two-man tent bending and straightening in the raging wind.

Within a few giant leaps and bounds, he was close to the tent within fifty metres and released another bone chilling howl. As the werewolf strode through the trees and bushes towards the clearing, it saw a man leave the tent holding a torch with a strong straight line of light, this illumination quivered on the ground by the surrounding pine trees. With another giant stride the werewolf closed in on his prey and with every stride the man's life expectancy drastically decreased.

The shaky beam of light rose up from the wood's floor and shone directly in the face of the snarling werewolf. His scream failed to escape his throat as it was choked by fear as he stood there paralysed. The beast swiped his abdomen spilling his intestine on the forest floor just by his trembling feet. The glistening snake orgy was illuminated for a brief second as the torch light bounced and then turned the scene into darkness. The man's other hand released an insufficient Swiss army pen knife and that too fell to earth. Just as the pen knife fell to earth, the ex-holder of it began his own flight as one back hand claw swipe sent him a height of forty feet up in the air and covered a distance of twenty feet. His now lifeless body crashed through the upper canopy of branches, leaves and foliage and fell in a tangled mess at the base of an oak tree close to the shivering tent.

The beast then strode towards the tent, as he did he could hear the racing heart-beat of the tent's occupant getting even faster. It reached down and clutched the tent's canopy and hurled it into the air. The quivering female left on the ground sheet uttered a few breathless words before another vicious right claw cut through bones, muscles, sinews and organs completely cutting the woman's body in two. Her legs kicked on their own until her remaining muscles moved for the last time. Then the werewolf howled again as it gorged itself on the fresh meat before it bounded off into the night.

Four hours had passed since the couple were brutally attacked and the first rays of dawn were peeping over the horizon therefore the werewolf stalking time had come to an end. His talons gripped the exposed slate of Crompton Moor's waterfall and its claws dug into the rock as the water cascaded down onto the red furred beast below. With one last howl the change happened and its claws retracted back into the older man's hands. Its furry muzzle shrunk and became Ken's screaming mouth, not from the pain of the change but the pounding freezing cold waterfall that he stood under. The hairy beast had now gone and only Ken was left clean washed from any blood splatter. He stood for a second under the waterfall unsure where he was but stepping out from under the spray, he recognised his own park where he had been coming since he was a child.

His tattered waterproof pants were all that remained of his clothing so he held the shreds of his jogging bottoms up with his hands and quickly made his way back to the wooded area where earlier he had tried in vain to subdue the werewolf. The scene sank his heart for one of the park's great oak trees lay whimpering and broken at the trunk. Its uppermost branches were being comforted by the surrounding trees resting as if recovering from a great trauma. The remnants of his ripped-up clothes were strewn across the scene. Ken proceeded to pick up his destroyed green jacket which was sliced beyond recognition. His shredded walking shoes were now in two halves, the sole and upper leather now separated. Hastily Ken had tried to remove any evidence that he was there at all. He managed to find his recently purchased crumpled hand cuffs and broken half rimmed spectacle. He had done the same clearing up operation the previous month when he could not have known that part of his tattered Park Ranger shirt was now being used as insulation for a female robin's nest. And that a particular piece of fabric which contained a CMR in front of an oak tree which to the casual observer might not mean much but to the well informed is the badge of the Crompton Moor Rangers. He grabbed whatever he could and quickly made his way back to his park lodge which was located close by on the edge of the park boundary down a short path.

He had managed to locate his binoculars and telescope before reporting the body of the two walkers that were found on the moors last month. This time he felt it would be better for someone else to stumble across the crime scene. He had only been back home for around ten minutes when the first of Crompton Moor visitors, an unfortunate young lady during her early morning jog made a horrendous discovery of another double homicide.

Chapter 8
Judge George Merrifield

Clayton Rudd winced as he stretched his left arm in front of his chest to finish the last loop of his double Windsor knot tie; it was a double Windsor knot kind of day. He felt relief as he let his left arm relax again and let his sling take the weight. Jessica had been to visit him several times since the shooting. She offered to move in to look after him, he thanked her for her concern but he was a big boy now and he would be okay. His whole left arm was still in bandages since the shotgun shooting two months previously. When he was rushed to The Royal Oldham Hospital where the doctors had managed to stem the bleeding and said that he was lucky not to lose his arm. They could not say when full fine motor skills would return back to normal but regular exercise was vital. He rolled his eyes when the consultant had suggested that learning the ukulele would help with his finger rehabilitation. "I came here to get better, not to get a new hobby," he joked.

The previous couple of months had been a frustrating time for him; firstly, he was off work due to his injuries, then two months later he was served papers because Billy Simpson died in custody although he was pronounced dead the scene. A full inquiry was held into the shooting. Naturally Clayton was suspended from duty while the inquiry was held, to be honest most of that time was spent recuperating in the hospital or at home. So, the suspension was just a red-tape formality.

After the death in custody inquiry, he had been completely

exonerated, indeed due to the number of independent witnesses who came forward and reported what he had done he became somewhat of a local hero who surely saved Jonathan's life. There was talk of the George Cross medal for bravery after he sacrificed himself for the child. He was embarrassed by all the attention and said that he was just trying to get close to Billy in order to disarm him.

Billy Simpson's brother and fellow accomplice Leroy was arrested at the scene and his trial had progressed quickly. Clayton was called to be a prosecution witness, detailing what he witnessed that day. The brave boy Jonathan was also called to give evidence through a signer.

Today was always coming, the day when the jury returned to deliver their verdict. He was really not looking forward to seeing the suspect Leroy Simpson again in court. There was something about killing a member of someone's family that always chilled the blood. Not to mention the fact he was being trialled for attempting to murder him.

Griffin Dunne rang the doorbell to One Heather Hill Clayton's house and stood waiting in the lightly lavender perfumed white porch area.

"Your chariot awaits, your majesty," said Griffin as he motioned with a sight bow and a wave of his hands towards his white Ford Sierra as Clayton opened his front door.

"Thanks, Griff, I didn't fancy getting bounced around in another black cab," said Clayton.

Both men got into Griffin's car and made the twenty-five-minute journey to Manchester Crown Court building. The imposing oval building with its white columns appeared from behind an office block with an air of majesty and authority that must have frightened any accused. Griffin and Clayton took their seat in the public gallery just as the large courtroom crackled with expectation when the defendant was brought into the dock and took his seat. The gallery was full of local and national pressmen waiting to write their scoop like vultures ready to pick over a carcass. The Simpson brothers, as they used to be called were notorious figures in the criminal underworld of greater Manchester. No one sold anything on the streets of North Manchester without giving them a cut and no one dared to do any hits without their say so. Normally when a court date was pending for any of the Simpson brothers then a vital witness would go missing or a jury member or two would suddenly disappear, so security had been significantly stepped-up.

The twelve members of the jury who were seated rose in unison as The Right Honourable Judge George Merrifield entered the courtroom. He was tall stocky man with an elderly face that still commanded respect. He wore a white permed wig that hung down to his shoulders which was adorned by his long flowing black and red robe.

"Please, be seated," said the court usher as the judge took his seat.

Over the previous five days, the jury had heard evidence from the defence and prosecution. They also heard the passionate closing statements from both the prosecution and defence barristers. Judge Merrifield then addressed the jury directly. "Foreman of the jury, have you all reached a decision that you are all agreed."

A nervous looking Asian man wearing a plain grey suit spoke directly to the judge. "Yes, your honour, we have reached a verdict."

"And this verdict, is it a unanimous one?" asked the judge.

"It is. your honour."

"Could we please hear your verdict?" asked the Judge.

The foreman then read from a sheet of paper "We the ladies and gentlemen of the jury find the accused Leroy Benjamin Simpson Guilty of attempted murder and guilty of armed robbery with grievous bodily harm.

There were cries and wailing from a small portion of the gallery where Leroy's mother and sister Ria were seated and a general commotion from the public gallery as the verdict was announced. Leroy himself just twisted his hands together and stared at the foreman of the jury. Clayton and Griffin simply shook hands as the judge addressed the defence barrister Mrs White QC.

"Are there any mitigating circumstances why Leroy Benjamin Simpson should not receive a custodial sentence?"

"Your honour, please before you pass judgement could I just make this appeal. Please don't let the manner of my client's arrest cloud your discussion. What we have here is a man that is grieving for the loss of his brother William Braden Simpson. The accused Mother Francesca Simpson is not only mourning the death of her baby son, William, but now she faces the real possibility of losing another one of her sons. Could we really inflict this ordeal on a woman in her late fifties? Don't forget that if we sentence this man today, we are also sentencing an innocent woman to a life sentence of loneliness. Surely, we could offer Leroy Simpson the chance for restorative justice. Let him meet his victims and see how his actions have impacted on them. Maybe this could turn around his life and become an upstanding citizen indeed a role model for his black community. Make others see that there is another way if you turn away from violence and crime," said Mrs Karen White QC.

"Thank you, Mrs White, for all those heart-felt words on

your client's behalf. Mr Simpson should at the very least realise that you have been a most excellent counsel for him and have done your utmost to serve his best interests. Unfortunately, I cannot allow any notions that your client may turn over a new leaf in the future and suddenly become, in your words, a role model or at the very least a decent man. I can only deal in facts not future possibilities and the facts as I see them are as follows. Yes, it is deeply regrettable that Mrs Francesca Simpson has recently lost one son, but that is no reason to spare Leroy a severe custodial sentence.

Judge Merrifield then addressed the whole of the courtroom. "I look upon you, Mr Simpson, and I don't see a single ounce of remorse in you at all. You were quite willing to use physical violence against members of the public with a total disregard for the consequences. You attempted to shoot a man at point blank range knowing that it could and probably would be fatal, especially after he already received a shotgun blow to the shoulder. My judgement in this case is that you are an evil man Mr Simpson and the general public need to be protected from your wicked nature. I, thereby, pronounce that you severe a minimum term of twenty years at her majesty's pleasure and no parole hearings will be entertained until that time has passed."

With the sentencing, Judge George Merrifield tapped his desk with his gavel and stood up. Just at that moment Leroy jumped from the dock and tried to make his way across the courtroom to where Clayton was sitting.

"You Bastard, you murdered my kid brother, don't think I won't find you, I'm coming for you, no prison is going to hold me, do you hear me I'm coming for you. I'm coming for you," shouted Leroy.

During his rant, three burly Group4 security guards grabbed

and pulled Leroy's six-foot 8 frame of muscle and rage towards a waiting prison van.

Clayton just stood there as he watched Leroy being dragged away. He had been threatened millions of times before, unfortunately it is the life of a Police officer but he had a cold feeling on the back of his neck, a feeling that just got deeper as he heard the last yells audible from the dragged Leroy.

"I'm coming for you, you hear me, you pig, I'm fucking coming for you!"

Chapter 9
Martin Fitzmaurice

When Clayton got to his desk inside the stone-coloured twin house design that was Greater Manchester Police station early that autumn morning, there was a post-it note slapped to his computer Monitor screen. **Meeting with Hannah, Nine a.m.** Griffin had the same note on his screen. It wasn't her usual way of getting attention, so something was definitely on her mind. He could already see Griffin who waited outside Hannah's office as he walked around the corner and took a seat outside. Both men chatted as they waited to be called in.

"Morning, Griff, what's this about then?" asked Clayton.

"Beats me, I just hope it doesn't impact on my leave next week, I'm taking Ruby and the kids to King's Lynn."

"You're the last of the jet sets, Griff," teased Clayton.

"If they play their cards right next year, it might be Blackpool!" joked Griff.

"I tell you what, Ruby hit the jackpot when she snared you." Clayton did an imaginary lasso pull around Griffin.

"Ouch." Clayton winced slightly when he did his lasso mime.

"Is you shoulder giving you jip?"

"Yeah, I forgot to take my pain killers, that's all," said Clayton.

"Well, that'll teach you to mock me." said Griffin.

Both men laughed as Hannah opened the door.

"Morning, gentlemen, please come in."

Both men stepped into the office and took a seat opposite Hannah.

"Clayton, Griff, I have asked you both to come in today because we have a pressing matter that needs urgent action. I am taking you off the Elizabeth Brook and Hazel Fry missing person inquiry just for the short term maybe a week or two, I want you to help with an ongoing investigation regarding the Crompton Moor killings. It is the strangest thing, a quiet rural community rocked by four horrific murders in the space of two months. Local Oldham police are still investigating but I want you two to read over their files and interview the witnesses. Maybe you will uncover something that they have missed. I have left the Crompton Moor files on your respective desks. Thank you, gentlemen, we'll have a meeting during the week to see how it is progressing."

They both stood up and began to make their way out as Hannah said, "Clay, thanks again for having Jess last weekend at such short notice. Mum was sick and Michael was away on one of his golfing weekends with the lads."

"No problem, I was her sous chef. We spent most of it improving my baking skills, we made cupcakes if I didn't like you so much I would have brought you one," said Clayton.

Hannah smiled as he closed the door to her office and returned to his.

Both Clayton and Griffin sat down at their desks and took out a pile of lose papers that were inside the case file, there were several colour and black and white photos of the murder scene. Clayton took out his notebook from his desk drawer and wrote down 'First thing: both attacks happened without any eye witnesses. Second; looking at the reports it seemed to involve some kind of animal attack as all the victims were torn apart with claws and teeth. Two months ago, the bodies of Albert and Dorothy Bradley were found by Ken Goodwin on his early morning rounds. Ken is the park ranger, a job he has been doing for thirty years, since leaving his position of lieutenant general in the Royal British Navy. Exactly one month later, the bodies of Sabu and Dimple Chopra were found by Joanne McCluskey while out jogging early in the morning of 12th August 1984.

"All I know, Griff, if we want to get to the bottom of all this we need to get to the scene and start asking questions, old school style in our Colombo Macs," said Clayton.

"'Ere, just one more question," said Griff in his best American accent.

They grabbed their coats and case files and headed to Griff's white Ford Sierra and drove the twenty-minute drive to Crompton Moor. They initially circled the moor trying to identify possible escape routes and identify all the secluded hiding spots of which there were a number. On the way to the far entrance adjacent to the hill adorned with the radio mast, they travelled along a remote country lane when they noticed a green Land Rover coming towards them. As both vehicles passed each other, the Land Rover driver wound down his window. A heavily bearded rugged looking man lent his head out to address the two detectives.

"Just be careful on your way up there, gentlemen, the stonewall on the bend has collapsed and there are some slates on the road," said the driver.

"Thank you, we'll keep our eyes peeled, my name is Inspector Rudd. Can I ask you if you're local to the area?" said Clayton. He took out his wallet and showed the man his police badge as Griffin did the same.

"Aye, I'm Martin Fitzmaurice and I run the farm and guest house just over the field in the next valley, Hawthorn Farm," said Martin.

"Would you mind if we ask you a few questions regarding the incidences over the last few months," said Clayton.

Martin nodded and both cars pulled over onto the gravel track and all three men got out and stood between their cars.

"So, what can you tell us about the incidents that have occurred here recently?" asked Griffin.

Martin looked at both the detectives and said, "Now if this is on the record then this will be a very brief conversation."

Both detectives looked at each other and then put their notepads back in their inside jacket pockets.

"I've been living on these hills around here man and boy for nearly eighty years and I thought I had seen and heard it all. But two months ago, my cattle were spooked, they were going crazy in the barn so I went to check on them, that's when I heard that howl coming from the woods. I thought that I had heard all the wildlife from around here foxes, ferrets and falcons. But I had never heard a howl with such menace and with such sinister overtones. I don't mind telling you that every hair on my body stood up. The full moon illuminated the whole of the moors on that clear evening. I remember seeing two figures disappearing over the brow and thinking it was getting a little late for walkers. A few moments later, I heard that blood curdling howl once again, this time louder and even more savage. I can tell you that I made sure all my animals were inside. The cows were in the barn and both of my dogs were inside. I don't mind telling you that I didn't get any sleep that night. I just sat in my kitchen chair with my 12-gauge shotgun loaded under my arm. When I heard the news about the double murders, I was shocked to hear about the utter savage violence but strangely I wasn't surprised. That

70

night there was a bad moon in the sky and it was the same last month. I can tell you that for nothing. I hadn't had a holiday or a day away from the farm in over twenty years and I never known the likes of it. Only recently have I started to leave the farm on occasions since my wife passed," Martin said.

"Sorry to hear that, when did your wife pass?" asked Griffin.

"My wife Eve, past four months ago she had been fighting a disease for the past few years until she finally succumbs. Since her passing, I no longer needed to be her carer, so last month I surprised my granddaughter who lives in Cornwall with a visit. I read the news of the camping couple in the National Paper a day or two later again this happened on a full moon night." Martin paused to pop a 'Fisherman's Friend' in his mouth.

"So, are you saying that this man only attacks during a full moon?" asked Griffin.

"The attacks only happen during full moons, but I never said anything about a man. What you've got here is your classic case of a Lycanthrope." Both Clayton and Griffin look at each other with a confused look on their face.

"In other words, a fucking werewolf," said Martin.

Again, Clayton and Griffin gave another look at each other; a silent message known only to them was passed between them. It is time they were going.

"Well, thank you for your time, Mr Fitzmaurice, we'll be in touch if we need any more information," said Griffin as he stepped forward and shook Martin's hand.

"I'm on my way out of here for a few days. There is a bad moon on the rise tonight," Martin said as he walked back to his Land Rover. He paused, looked at the gloomy overcast sky, which hung above the vast expanse of ancient woodlands and said under his breath, "Yes, there is a bad moon on the rise."

Chapter 10
Griffin Dunne

Clayton and Griffin sat in silence in their car and waited for Martin's Land Rover to disappear around the bend. Then Griffin said, "I can see why you didn't want to go on the record." At which point both men broke into fits of laughter. "I've bloody heard it all now; a bloody werewolf killed all those people," said Clayton.

Griffin wiped the little bit of moisture that had gathered in his left eye and sighed deeply as the last of his laughter died away.

"Come on, Clayton, let's look for clues in the bloody real world, we'll look around the murder scene while we still have the natural light."

The two detectives approached the scene where Sabu and Dimples' bodies were found. The last of the police tape had been taken down and the patches of blood had long since dried up. As the two detectives surveyed the scene, they could see where the tree had fallen and disturbed the surrounding woodland. The park's tree surgeon had already cleaned up and the splintered oak tree had been removed but branches and some of loose foliage were left where they fell. The destruction of the tree and the brutal murders was still unclear if they were linked somehow. Unfortunately, the felling of the tree had disturbed a robin's nest which was snugly hid away on one of the uppermost branches but now lay abandoned on the side of a beech tree trunk with two blue eggs still inside. The two detectives stopped and looked closely at the makeup of the nest. Griffin noticed that intertwined in the twigs and leaves was a piece of material that was wholly out of place, it was a piece of dirty white fabric with an oak tree behind the letters CMR.

"Clay, come here and take a look at this, it looks like the insignia of the Crompton Moor Rangers. Wasn't it the ranger who found murdered walkers if I'm not mistaken. Now I'm not suggesting that a seventy-year-old brutally murdered those people for an instant but something has been overlooked here. There are little things that just don't quite add up in my head. It is just something that I can't quite put my finger on," said Griffin.

"I know what you mean, I think a little more attention needs to be paid to Mr Goodwin. Let's go and have a chat with him and see if his alibi really does hold water," said Clayton.

Both men began to contemplate their plan of attack when they talked to Ken. So, they talked strategy as they made their way back to Griff's Ford Sierra and drove to Ken Goodwin's home address.

Ken's small cottage was situated on the side of a grassy hill up a country lane that ran adjacent to Brushes Clough Reservoir on the edge of Crompton Moor. On reaching his house, they were informed by his wife Charlotte that Ken was on the last of his rounds. After what went on over the previous months, he was making sure that no one was still in the park after nightfall. There were only a few hours of daylight left so Griff and Clayton made the decision that they will meet Ken as he finished his round to ask him a few questions.

"I knew today was going to be a long day, I better ring Ruby and tell her that I'll be late for tea," said Griff.

"That's police work for you, no respecters of schedules,"

said Clayton.

The early autumn sun was low in the sky as the long shadows of the trees created a contrast of bright and dark stretched on the forest floor, so each step was a step into the blinding crimson sun and the sudden darkness of the opaque tree trunks. Nevertheless, the two detectives made their way back to Crompton Moor and walked back into the deserted woods. They could see where Ken had parked his yellow motorised bicycle in the deserted sandy car park. All was quiet as a female tawny owl silently swooped low and through the long grass looking for an unfortunate field mouse to feed to her hungry owlets.

The pair of detectives walked cautiously amongst the pine trees, slowly getting used to the varying levels of light until they entered a clearing in the centre of the trees. Griff and Clayton suddenly noticed a figure sitting in the distance. As they plodded closer through the long spiky grass, they could see that it was Ken Goodwin sat at the far end of the clearing with his back to the approaching men. The fallen pine leaves scattered all around create a soft carpet of silence where even heavy footsteps were softened. So, Ken had no idea that the two figures had entered the clearing only twenty feet behind him. As they approached their anxiety levels slowly increased with each passing step because there was something eerie about this situation. He sat hunched on a boulder and had something on his lap that periodically caught a ray of sun and illuminated the tree trunk opposite with shards of light.

"Ken, are you okay?" Clayton called out as they made their way to his position.

Ken turned to see where the voice had come from, he looked like he had just woken up from a deep sleep or had been crying because both his eyes were swollen.

"You shouldn't be here now," he said as he put the object that he was fidgeting with in his pocket.

"Hello Ken, I am Detective Inspector Dunne and this is my colleague, Inspector Rudd, could we just have a moment of your time," said Griffin.

"Well, I'm afraid that's the one thing that I haven't got any more of... time," said Ken as he pulled back out a 'Smith & Wesson' Magnum Revolver out of his pocket.

Both Clayton and Griff hit the deck and dived behind a tree stump and a boulder respectively. Clayton behind the tree stump shouted, "Ken put the gun down and we can talk."

"Don't worry, the bullet in this gun is meant for no one else but me," replied Ken.

"Whatever has happened, we'll hear your side and we can help you! Just drop the gun," shouted Griffin.

"You can't help me; no one can help me now. Please just let me kill myself before other people are killed, I can't live with myself I don't want anyone else to suffer this is the only way out," shouted Ken through the lump growing in his throat.

He then reached into his inside pocket and pulled out an envelope with the name 'Lottie' written on it. He dropped it on the ground near where he stood.

"Please make sure, Charlotte gets this letter. I was going to leave it for her but I was scared that she would find it before I left," said Ken, his voice was so much softer now as his eyes glazed over and filled with tears.

Maybe it was his teary eyes or the numbness of his body as the realisation of what he was about to do but Ken didn't notice the stealthy crawl of Clayton. Clayton winched through his shoulder pain as he slowly circled around the back of Ken keeping his body low while Griffin kept him talking.

"Why do you want to end your life, Ken, things are never that bad," asked Griffin.

A wry smile inched onto Ken's face.

"Ha never that bad, you haven't seen the thing that I become and the bad things that happen... talking about bad things happening I have nearly run out of time the moon is nearly at its peak in the sky," said Ken.

Clayton and Griffin had not noticed how the sun had disappeared behind the grassy hills and now the three men stood in the late dusk light.

Ken, suddenly, stood up and announced talking time was over. He then lifted the gun to his right temple but just before he could pull the trigger Clayton jumped on him from behind sending the revolver hurtling out of his grasp and into a pile of scattered pine needles.

Just at that moment, the large crimson moon was visible through the branches and leaves of the forest canopy. He was still on top of Ken holding him down as Clayton reached for his belt and his ratchet style handcuffs. At seventy-eight years old Ken didn't put up much of resistance when Clayton knocked him down and was fairly easy to keep subdued but suddenly Ken began to stand up slow and steady. Clayton found himself powerless to stop the rising Ken from getting to his feet, like trying to stop a lift from going up just by stamping on the floor.

An entranced, heavily breathing Ken slowly stood bolt upright as Clayton tried again to knock him down. This time when he jumped on Ken's back half expecting his body weight to send him crashing to the ground but that didn't happen. He just stood there solid as a rock. He desperately tried to bring him down using a choke hold with his forearm against Ken's throat and locked in tight with his other already aching arm. The firmness got tighter and tighter as Ken's neck seemed to expand and Clayton had the strangest feeling that his feet were slowly rising in the air. The back of Ken's head which was mostly scalp and the finest of grey hairs suddenly was being covered in thick red coarse fur. Clayton's brain did not have time to register this impossible occurrence when a giant claw came around his side and pierced his back through his jacket and shirt. The five talons drew blood as they ripped into his flesh. The next second the claw had thrown him through the air like a toddler throwing a teddy bear in a tantrum.

Clayton crashed into the gnarled roots of a sycamore tree. His face was grazed from sliding along the course ground and his body ached from the force that he was thrown through the air. His back was stinging as if five knives were sticking in him. Through the pain and confusion, he turned his head and saw Ken clothing split from his body and a red hairy beast forced its way out. A muzzle full of drooling fangs and furious green eyes had now replaced Ken downtrodden face.

Griffin after initially running to help Clayton apprehend Ken had now froze in horror as he saw Ken morph into something from a nightmare right in front of him. He screamed for help but it was caught in his throat as the werewolf sprung at Griffin ripping out his windpipe and breaking open his ribcage to gauge on his warm organs inside. His life slowly ebbed away with every crunch of the werewolf's powerful jaw. The whole attack took less than five seconds before the beast stood up from the gooey mess that used to be Detective Inspector Griffin Dunne.

It howled as the blood fell from its muzzle. Its head then turned violently to locate the floundering Clayton who had just managed to pull himself up onto his feet. As the werewolf looked straight at him with its snarling face his legs gave way and he collapsed back onto the pine needle covered ground. As he fell back his arm reached out into the darkness to break the impact of his fall when his right hand landed on something hard lying amongst the soft pine needles.

With drool dropping from the beast's muzzle the werewolf took one giant step towards the grounded man. Clayton twisted the half-buried revolver so that he could grip the handle and felt for the trigger. The feel of the gun did not bring any comfort to him as his heart beat so fast he felt as if he was going to pass out. The beast crouched slightly before springing through the air, jaws opened claws outstretched. Without thinking, Clayton swung his arm and squeezed the trigger. A flash of light illuminated the leaping werewolf in mid-air and an ear-splitting explosion cracked as the bullet left the gun. It entered between the werewolf's eyes ripping a massive hole and exited from the back of its head with a large chunk of its brain in tow. The beast crashed to the floor only a few feet away from Clayton's outstretched legs.

A muffled low-pitched whine was heard from the stricken beast and then silence. Clayton watched in horror and amazement as the werewolf's bones started to shorten and its red hair began to retract until the body of a half-naked seventy-eight-year-old ranger lay face down in front of him. Using all the strength Clayton had left he stumbled over to the remains of Griffin. Under normal protocol he would have checked for a pulse but the lack of a jaw and neck left that option redundant. He then somehow managed to stumble back to the police radio in the car and managed to get out one sentence before collapsing from extreme blood loss.

"Urgent assistance needed at Crompton Moor Country Park... officer down."

Chapter 11
Maggie Hurst

Margaret Hurst brushed a stray red hair out of her face and focused her eye piece to sharpen the image of the piece of metal as she looked through the microscope in her ballistics forensic lab. She then used her Vernier callipers to accurately measure the cartridge case and then jotted something down in her notebook under 'Calibre'. In all her twelve years of working in the forensic science department, she had never had a case that had been so close to home. Her colleague and friend Griffin Dunne had been found ripped to pieces; it was the most disturbing scene she had ever worked on. Just when she thought she had seen it all.

Margaret gently squeezed the pipit of Sulphur Chlorite on the piece of blackened metal and observed how it hissed and emitted a small degree of vapour. The fragment of bullet under the microscope fizzed while being manipulated by Margaret's tweezers. She picked up her pocket-sized dicta-phone pressed record and spoke into the microphone as the tiny tape wheel rotated. After a full examination, she placed the piece of twisted metal into a clear bag and sealed it. After writing another brief message, she closed her notebook entitled 'Forensic Gunshot Residue Analysis' and walked over to her laboratory telephone and dialled a number. Impatiently she tapped the side of the black phone as the dial slowly rotated back. She waited to speak to someone but the phone just rang without anyone picking up at the other end, she sighed and hung up the receiver.

Clayton rolled over as the glint of sunshine shone through the tiniest crack between his curtain and his window. It was mid-afternoon and he was still in bed. The difference between night and day failed to register to him at that moment. He was still in mourning from the killing of his long-time colleague and friend.

It was so hard to take, thinking that Griffin had been killed. Griffin had taken him under his wing when he first joined the force and had been like a father figure to him especially after his own father had died. He was there when things had gone sour with Hannah. He thought back to the time when Griff had taken him out for a drink and said to him "You don't have to marry someone because you got them pregnant, you have only just started seeing her" but Clayton had wanted to do the right thing and in hindsight Griffin was probably right. Yes, it is fair to say that Griff was more like family to him. So, his heart felt like it had been ripped out when he saw Ruby Dunne and the kids at the funeral. He couldn't help feeling that somehow, she blamed him for Griffin's death. Which in turn made him question himself; could he have done anything different? His police training had always told him to expect the unexpected but they never covered what to do if the seventy-eight-year-old man that you were arresting suddenly turned into a blood-thirsty werewolf.

Internal affairs and the Chief Coroner both conducted separate inquiries into the double homicide at Crompton Moor and they could not conclude as to how both men died. There wasn't enough evidence to conclude that Clayton was not acting in self-defence when he took the fatal shot that killed Ken Goodwin. The death of both men was filed as unexplained after the two-week long investigation.

Hannah Baker was left in a difficult position but she had no choice but to suspend Clayton on full pay until the findings from the investigation were disclosed. Needless to say, that the coroner had to order a drug test on Clayton when he claimed that Griff was attacked by a wild animal and Ken Goodwin was a midnight nudist with murderous tendencies!

Chief Inspector Baker had come around to his house to speak to him two days ago to tell him that he could return to work because the unexplained death verdict meant that no criminal charges could be brought by the Crown Prosecution Service. She also suggested that even though he could return to work maybe he should take another few weeks off and try to get his head together before setting foot back there. Before he went back to work 'ha' that's a joke. Clayton was all too aware of what he was now after what he saw on that night. He was now the ultimate killing machine and the next full moon since his attack was tomorrow night. If the theories about werewolves were correct then anyone who survived an attack from one would become a werewolf on the next full moon? Could he take that chance? What if he hurt his loved ones? That was one risk he couldn't take. He rubbed one of the five claw scars that were embedded on his back with his fingertips and could feel the raised scar marks on his skin. The claw scratches were spread out covering the whole edge of his back such was the size of the huge beast's claw.

Clayton now had to have some time to deliberate, a deliberation that tragically thousands of young men have had: How to kill yourself? It was a thought that he obviously did not want to be have especially as a Roman Catholic, suicide was a cardinal sin. *But what alternative did he have?* As a lot people know there is nothing like drinking yourself into near oblivion to help procrastination and putting things off that you know you need to do.

He completed another turn on his bed and reached up to his bedside table for another shot of 'Jack Daniels'. Maybe not so much of a shot more like a large gulp straight from the bottle. Shakily he brought the bottle to his lips and his heart sank when he realised that he had already drunk that particular bottle dry. He sighed and winced as he hauled himself upright in bed. The effort needed to sit up in bed felt more like a gruelling gym session. Sat up in bed he then gingerly hauled himself to the kitchen for a fresh bottle of his new best friend Mr Daniels.

The phone rang as he entered the kitchen, he contemplated letting it ring out like he did the previous five times. Maybe because he was already on his feet or the volume of the bell sounded so much louder when his head wasn't on his pillow that each ring felt like an electric shock to his brain. The only way to silence the ringing was to answer it. He picked up his black receiver, held it to his ear and closed his eyes with a pained expression on his face.

"Ah, hello, Clayton here," he whispered.

"Hello, Clayton, thank god you picked up, it's me Maggie, how are you? Are you coping?" asked Margaret.

"I'm not at the moment, Maggie, I just need some more time to get my head straight."

"Well, I wanted you to know that I have some information about the… incident," she said.

"I'm all ears, Maggie, I would love some more good news," yawned Clayton.

"Funny, Clay, anyway the bullet fragment taken from the scene which appeared to enter and exit Ken Woodwin's cranium is not made from a usual ammunition metallic compound. The bullet had traces of Argentite and Chlorargyrite," stated Margaret.

"Maggie, please could I have that again, this time in English," said Clayton.

"In other words, it was a silver bullet!" said Margaret.

"Silver bullet maybe he was a massive Lone Ranger fan," said Clayton.

"You don't sound that surprised, Clay," said Maggie.

"I guess I'm just a little under the weather or perhaps a little over refreshed," he said.

There were a few moments of silence before Clayton thanked Maggie and hung up the phone. That was great news now if he wanted to kill himself he had to get hold of a silver bullet before tomorrow night. Which was going to be almost impossible and there was no way of killing a werewolf without a silver bullet. But then a thought occurred to him. Maybe instead of killing the werewolf and obviously killing himself, there might be another way. What if there was a way to contain the beast. And a way to contain the beast was literally right under his nose.

He dragged his drunken limps over towards the now dusty bookcase and placed a wayward finger on 'The Strange Case of Dr Jekyll and Mr Hyde' book. He rubbed the dust on his fingertips together as they flaked down, he thought he must give the bookcase a thorough dusting. The next thought that went through his mind was, *Maybe it is time to dust off the underground bunker too.*

Chapter 12
Clayton Rudd

Clayton woke up early on Thursday morning; it was the day of the full moon. This was going to be a decisive day one way or another. First job of the day was to clean the whole of his house, because it had the appearance that it had been overtaken by a bunch of squatters. Also, he decided he had to say good-bye to his new best friend Jack Daniels for a while because a clear head today was a must. The next few hours were spent vacuuming, dusting, polishing and scrubbing. There was no way that his house if it was going to be a potential crime scene was going to look like a shit hole.

There were only two hours to go before the moon was due to rise. So, he sat down in his recently restored show home to consume his freshly roasted lamb dinner. It had always been his favourite meal; the slow roasted lamb, slightly pink in the middle, light fluffy oven roasted potatoes, Julienne carrots dripping in salty butter, crunchy Brussels sprouts good all year round and topped with burgundy wine infused thick rich gravy. As he enjoyed the very last morsel and placed his cutlery on his plate, he sat back in his chair and thought that sure was better for him than all those liquid lunches recently.

Barely had he finished off the last of his Shiraz when the front doorbell rang. He opened it to find of all people the people in the world Michael Baker, his ex-wife's new husband, standing in his porch way carrying two shopping bags.

"Oh hello, Michael, this is a surprise," said Clayton.

"Oh hi, Clayton. Hannah asked me to get a few things for you. She said that Maggie had said that you have been moping around at home for the last few weeks and she was worried about you," said Michael.

"You can tell Hannah and Maggie that I am fine but thank you for the groceries. I hope you didn't go to any trouble," said Clayton.

"Oh no, bother, it's nothing really just some bread, milk, bacon and a four pack of Hofmeister the bare essentials, no pun intended," joked Michael.

"Follow the bear I get it. Once again cheers Mike," said Clayton.

Michael handed the bags of groceries over as Clayton asked, "How is Jessica doing?"

"She's fine. She and Hannah have gone down to London for a bit of mother and daughter time, wasting money on Oxford Street no doubt. Anyway, I've got a few days to kill before they get back, so I might check out that new movie 'Ghostbusters' at the Roxy," said Michael.

"Nice one, well thanks again for the bread and milk and enjoy the movie," said Clayton as he said bye to Michael.

He watched as Michael climbed into his dark blue BMW 7 series and drove down the hill and disappeared around the corner.

The early evening sky was still and cloudless as Clayton closed his porch door and locked his front door with the double bolt lock. He methodically walked around the whole of his house and made sure that each door and window was closed and secure. He turned down the lights in his house and finally pulled 'The Strange Case of Dr Jekyll and Mr Hyde' book and the whole bookcase slid forward. A fresh breeze cooled his face as the bookcase sprung forward and revealed the staircase that led down to the underground bunker.

As he gradually descended the stairs the motion capture sensors automatically activated the lights as he approached. The main light then illuminated the holding room at the bottom where the thick metal door was already opened. He walked to the control panel which was embedded in the door. It simply showed a dial for how long after the door was locked before it was able to be opened again from the inside. Uncle Patrick built in this extra feature to stop anyone opening the door before all the radioactive particles had dissipated. Clayton turned the dial to ten hours. *That should take me way into tomorrow morning before the door automatically opens.* He chuckled to himself when he noticed that the maximum setting was one hundred years.

He stood still and took a very deep breath and then pressed the large red button on the inside wall to close the door shut. With a screech of metal that had not moved in years the heavy door swung closed with a loud thud that echoed inside the vault room. Then seven metal rods instantly locked into place. After the scrape of metal against metal, there was only a deafly silence until the gentle hum as the air conditioning kicked in.

A long strip light glowed gently until it slowly heated up and illuminated the books, bed and bathroom door. Now locked in the bunker Clayton did not know what to do with himself. *Would anything happen, would he even change? And if he did would the bunker be strong enough to contain the werewolf?* All of these questions would soon be answered but the only thing he knew for sure now was that he was doing everything he possibly could.

He sat on his single bed, then lay down, but his mind was far too active for sleep. He just lay there looking up at the dancing halogen light. Who knows how long it took for sleep to eventually come to him but it did not last for long. He was thrust out of bed as if being catapulted by a giant invisible piece of elastic. Standing bolt upright his back cracked twisted and stretched. His head was flung back as he let out a yell of pain as his jaws started to protrude from his face and turned into a wolf's muzzle. The yell of pain was strangled and it became a howl. Black fur suddenly grew from every one of his pours, as his t-shirt and jeans tightened under his rapidly expanding muscles. The denim and cotton were no match for the force of the muscle growth as they split and shredded into ribbons. Clayton's feet were no longer feet but giant claws with razor sharp talons cutting into the black and white lino. The giant beast looked at his huge claws that a few moments ago were hands. And just like that the change was complete as another guttural howl echoed around the bunker. The humongous werewolf stood still for less than a second after the change was complete then it leapt across the room and smashed into the three feet thick titanium door with a force that would have ripped through any normal door or even solid brick wall but not this door. The huge beast growled and howled with rage as it flung it half a tonne of weight at the door but it did not budge, just squeaked slightly under the viscous assault. The pounds on the door were relentless for over an hour as the werewolf tried to escape and satisfy its bloodlust, but in vain as the door would not yield.

Eventually, the rest of the room paid for the werewolf's rage at its incarceration. The single bed mattress was ripped in two with a single swipe of its claw sending a blizzard of coloured foam into the air which landed and covered the naked bed frame. Mangled springs hung like entrails as it was tossed across the room. The beast brought down its foot onto the bed's metal headboard crumpling it like it was made from papier-mâché.

The carnage continued as the bookshelf joined the mattress flung across the room, duck egg blue toilet bowl and cistern was ripped out of the wall flooding the floor with blue chemical waste. The werewolf then picked up the treadmill and threw it into the kitchen scattering the tins of beans. The thick red goo splashed on the floor and collected at the shower plug.

The rage and fury within the beast did not dissipate for hours while the creature remained, but eventually as the sky outside lightened and the power and pull of the moon slowly diminished, the werewolf fell to the floor and began to transform back into Clayton. His arms and legs slowly shrunk back to their original size, the dark black hair retreated along with his excessive muscular physique. As the last remnants of the beast vanished, it left Clayton exhausted in a deep sleep on the floor just as the internal timer in the door registered ten hours and clicked, suddenly all of the titanium bolts retracted and the massive door opened automatically.

He woke, opened his eyes to the utter destruction of the underground bunker, but strangely the wrecked room actually was a relief as he realised that the bunker door must have contained the beast. He smiled he felt great even his injured shoulder that ached the previous day felt brand new. He wiped the build-up of sleep from his eyes and the only thought that filled his head was he may just have found clemency from his death sentence. *It is the biggest relief in anyone's life when suicide is not the only answer.* Suddenly, the thought of suicide seemed so distant like a different life-time, not just from the previous day.

Chapter 13
Hawthorn Farm

The late evening sun shone a hazy crimson against the fluffy white spring-time clouds. It silhouetted the figure of Martin Fitzmaurice as he stood for a moment or two outside his large black and grey barn. His muddy green boots seemed reluctant to move from their position in the squelchy mud. It wasn't the chilly breeze that created the slight tremor in his calloused, wrinkled hands as he gripped the iron padlock. A turn of the key and the barn was secured for the night or as secure as he could possibly make it.

He breathed deeply and turned away from the barn and trudged through the sloppy mud towards his farmhouse. On entering the bare brick kitchen, he was greeted by shrill tones of the phone ringing in the living room. A cursory drag of both feet was all the effort Martin made to clean his mud crusted dark green boots before walking to the dimly lit living room, and picked up the phone.

"Hello, Hawthorn Farm," he said.

"Hello, Martin, is that you? It's Ken."

"Oh, hello, Ken, how are you keeping? How can I help you?"

"I'm good. Thanks, Martin, I was just wondering if you're free tonight. We have had some trouble recently with poachers stealing bird eggs and I recently discovered a Tawny Owl nesting site on the outskirts of Crompton wood. I just wanted to do a midnight check and was seeing if you fancy joining me. I'll bring the coffee laced with your favourite scotch," said Ken.

"Ha ha, Ken, you do paint a very tempting offer, but I can't make it tonight. Eve is having one of her funny turns, so I need to keep an eye on her," answered Martin.

"No worries, friend, you take good care of that lady of yours and get her back on her feet soon," said Ken.

"Thanks, Ken, and you take care too, will see you soon. Bye."

"I'll pop up to see you two in a few days, bye," said Ken.

Martin hung up the phone on the receiver and went into the kitchen. He opened the ornate wooden carved cupboard, took out a short crystal tumbler and poured himself a very generous measure of 'Famous Grouse' whiskey. Carefully, he then opened up his rifle display which dominated the space above the kitchen's fireplace. Pulled a drawer underneath the display cabinet and took out some ammunition, loaded two shiny cylinders into the shotgun's chamber and took the gun to his living room armchair.

Martin held his 12-bore shotgun with both hands as he slowly rocked back and forth in his rocking armchair for an hour or two. The soft moonlight illuminated his wrinkled brow and eyes. His face was pained with anguish as he listened to the thuds, thumps and howls which were now coming from the barn. The knuckles on his wrinkled right hand had turned white as he gripped the shotgun harder with every thump. He had followed the same routine; the shotgun had to be loaded with the special ammo at this time of the month and every month for the past three years, pure Sterling silver. The growls were something that he had heard many times but yet each time it was a slash to his soul as he winced with every howl. The thrashing sound was constant until suddenly it stopped! His wincing face suddenly froze and was replaced by one of utter horror for he knew that the beast was out.

Now another sound split the night air, screams and grunts of pigs and sheep being slaughtered as the beast ran amok. Martin leapt up from his chair like a flea on a scabby dog and bolted out of the farmhouse. He was short of breath as he ran the well-worn path across to the barn. The once secure barn now had a massive opening; the aluminium side had exploded with a giant star hole revealing a silver cage with a crumpled door hanging by one hinge.

"Shit... No!"

He cursed then grumbled to himself he knew he should have invested in another silver-plated cage; how could it take all that abuse and punishment without eventually yielding. He felt like a fool, the silver which coated the bars acted as an effective repellent to the creature's jaws and teeth but eventually the cold damp barn would contribute to its corrosion and, therefore, it lost its impermeable properties. *How could he put financial considerations before safety?*

Martin knew he had to think fast so jumped on his quad bike still with a bale of hay strapped to the rear and instantly pursued the beast. It was easy to see which way it went just by viewing the line of slaughtered livestock heading towards Crompton Moor and towards Ken Goodwin!

The light of the full moon was the main source of light as the dark sky gave Crompton Woods more than an element of menace, as the Martin's quad bike leaped over the exposed roots and the occasional molehill which made for a decidedly bumpy ride.

In a clearing in the woods, Martin could see Ken Goodwin

in his all green outfit, he was unmistakable even in the low moonlight. The only thought that occupied his mind was he must get to him and get him away from any harm before the beast could strike. The hum of the approaching quad bike was drowned out by a high-pitched howl that emitted from the close-by woods as a huge grey werewolf leaped from out of the trees. Ken on hearing the howl turned around and lost his footing on the uneven ground, he still received a glancing blow from the grey wolf's right claw. The hard blow knocked him over because he fell like a sack of potatoes with a thud. The impact of the ground had twisted his knee under his body weight. His torso and his head hit the grassy ground with a force that knocked him out cold.

The huge grey shaggy werewolf instantly turned to finish off the unconscious Ken. The beast lifted a claw just as silver buckshot ripped through its stomach and sent it back. It collapsed against the trunk of a Cherry Blossom tree in full bloom. The thud against the trunk shook the blossom that fell like pink snowflakes and covered the ground. The werewolf howled in pain as the poisonous silver coursed through its innards melting everything it touched, turning its blood to red vapour. Then suddenly, the wailing and howling stopped and the night was still. Discharged smoke from the shotgun mingled with night's mist as Martin's right arm collapsed and let the barrel swing down.

He did not have time to contemplate what had just happened. First things first, he dragged and heaved the unconscious Ken onto the back of his quad bike by doing so dislodging the bale of hay. He then transported him to The Royal Oldham Hospital, where managed with great excursion to drag him to the main entrance and left him there to be found and looked after. He waited in the far car park until he saw a nurse leaving after her late shift. Dimple Chopra stopped when she saw the stricken man lying outside the main entrance and imminently bent down to take his pulse. When she found that he was still alive, she instantly raised the alarm and within moments the crash team was on the scene assisting the badly injured Ken.

Martin felt satisfied that Ken was now in the best hands and made his way back to Crompton Moor Woods. Tears filled his eyes as he went to the spot where the werewolf had fallen but now the grey hair, claws and fangs had retracted and the beast had long gone, leaving a dead naked seventy-year-old lady, adorned with blossom, lay slumped where the werewolf had fallen.

He jumped off his quad bike and caressed the lifeless body of his wife, which lay at the base of the cherry blossom tree surround by a bed of wild poppies.

"My Eve. Eve, my love, please forgive me... your suffering has ended now, my love... now you can rest."

The lifeless face of his wife looked serene and at peace as a tear dropped from Martin's eye and landed on her cheek. He then gripped his naked wife's body with his strong, hard-working arms and held her close in an embrace as he shook and cried out again. "I'm sorry... I'm sorry, please forgive me..."

His wails of grief eventually died away as the full moon slowly set over the now deathly quiet Crompton Moor.

Chapter 14
Ellie Tierney

The light brown Fiat Argenta changed lanes as it came off the A666 on its way from Manchester to Bolton. The driver was a man of medium build with a short trimmed beard framing his thin face. It gave him the look of a man several years older than twenty-five. This relatively short journey had been one full of irritation for him. Not just his newly acquired itchy 'Jack Nicolson' tattoo with his menacing, smiling face, hot and sticky under the double-wrapped cling film. The main discomfort came from a feeling that he was about to do something wrong, something that would bring pain to others, but yet he felt a compulsion that would not subside. It was a feeling like a compulsive gambler going to a casino knowing that he shouldn't but wanting the thrill. It was a feeling that was growing inside him over the last few years. It was an itch that was finally going to be scratched tonight.

He knew exactly where to go in order to satisfy his craving, a quiet industrial estate, where mostly the people hanging around on the street at that time of night were ladies from an Eastern European country, with their large locks of curly hair and that stern angular stare that seemed to say no time wasters. They all looked at the man as he turned right and passed their corner. The man did not stop for any of them because these ladies always worked under the supervision of their ever-watchful pimp.

Only a few minutes' drive up the road was a much more

appetising target, a solo girl standing under a street lamp. Her pink mini skirt stood out against her black tights and high heeled stilettoed shoes. She slightly bent over as the car slowed to a crawl, while taking a drag from her nearly finished cigarette.

"Looking for business tonight, sweetheart?" asked the woman in her North-West accent as the last resemblance of her smoke escaped from the corner of her baby pink lips.

"Yes, yes, please... you look really cute," said the man as he wound down his window a little wider.

"Okay, you charmer." The woman flicked the rest of her cigarette onto the pavement and walked round the front of the car and slid in the passenger side door.

"Keep driving, I know a good spot," she said as she motioned him to drive on. Soon, they left the dimly lit back streets of this particular red light district behind and were soon on a patch of wasteland behind Burnden Park Stadium, the local ground of Bolton Wanderers FC. Darkness surrounded the stadium as the wasteland stretched out into the void with only the council high-rise buildings on the horizon that gave off any additional light. The wild expanse had remnants of a gravel track which had served a building that had long been demolished. Nature had cultivated the rest with wild blackberry bushes whose fruit remained mostly unpicked by human hand; the majority was to be gauged on by the field mice or a passing fox.

As the brown Fiat Argenta car slowed down, the tyres crunched on the loose gravel, a grazing colony of rabbits scarpered and their eyes briefly reflected in the headlight as they leapt into the darkness.

The young lady motioned to the right hand-side of the car to a dark, silhouetted building.

"You can see the stadium from here. They are a real bag of shite, I'm the only one who scores round here, they had better get their act together or it won't just be me going down." The woman let out a high-pitched squeal as she said the punch line on her feebly joke.

The man thought, *I wonder how many times she has cracked that same joke to her punters*, and then noticed the youthful spark in her heavy, made up eyes.

"You seem really young to be doing this sort of thing," said the man.

"I'm twenty-two, but don't worry, I won't bore you with some sob story. I just want to make some easy money, that's all; why should I be collecting glasses and pulling pints all day in a sweaty bar. Guys are always trying to get their hands on my tits, so they may as well pay for the privilege. Name's Ellie, by the way," said Ellie as she smiled over to the man and motioned with her head.

"There is a bush over there, we can go there if you fancy."

The man stopped the car near a cluster of bushes. The metallic crunch of the handbrake was more pronounced as the engine died. He left the car with a squeak of the driver's door and crunched on the gravel stones as he walked to the rear of the car. A tiny insignificant light barely illuminated the contents of the car's boot as he opened it up. Underneath an old bag of golf clubs next to the car jack and a discoloured blue inhaler was a white carrier bag. He picked up the bag and took out its content which was a large brand-new chopper with a wooden handle and metallic blade. Ellie got out of the car and walked to the back where she, suddenly, froze as she saw the man standing with the chopper twisting slowly in his hand.

"Do you know what time it is? It's running time!" said the man.

Ellie screamed as the man took a step towards her. She turned and ran into the darkness away from the ambient light. Even though Ellie wore heels, she took off at a speed an Olympic sprinter would find hard to match. There is nothing like the fear of death that can get your muscles working overtime.

As Ellie's pink mini skirt tried to dissolve into the darkness, the man pursued her with the chopper raised high, level with his head. Her dark jacket and tights completely blended with the night, almost impossible to see at all. Only her pink mini skirt could betray her position. The man sprinted frantically, doing his best to follow as she ran towards the brambles and wild blackberry bushes. Then she completely disappeared without a trace.

"I'm gonna gut you like a fish, you bitch, you better come out!" shouted the man as he slashed wildly into the brambles and bushes, sending thorny canes into the air. Then he crashed through the bushes desperately trying to find the woman's hiding spot.

In his blind rage, he had not noticed that Ellie had crawled deep into the bushes with the thorns scratching at her hands, knees and ripping at her hair. She did not dare breathe as the chopper slashed the brambles and thicket just above her head. She could hear the tear as his trousers ripped when they snagged against the thorns. This did not stop him as he walked through the bushes, hunting her down.

Ellie knew that she could not take a chance that he wouldn't eventually find her in the undergrowth, so she had to make another run for it. She crawled out through the other side of the bushes and sprinted in the darkness back the way she had come where the car was parked. The man must have heard her rustling in the undergrowth and started to give chase once again.

"You're dead meat, bitch," shouted an angry voice in the darkness.

Ellie was getting away and thought she could use his own car to leave him behind, but without warning her foot slipped on the uneven stones. The man then closed the gap and did not waste any time in silencing her with a blow to the top of the head, sending a stream of blood squirting everywhere: across the dusty stones, onto his own face and across the left rear wheel of his parked car. The man's chopper blows rained down on the girl's body like a deadly jackhammer pounding her flesh.

For the briefest of seconds, he ceased his frenzied attack and turned his attention to her blood-covered left hand. He violently hacked it off on the third brutal strike.

Then punched the lifeless hand several times, sending blood oozing from the severed wrist, splattering the top of his trousers and onto the dead-still Ellie. After the final blow to the severed hand, he threw it into the open boot of his car. Something in his head told him now was his chance to get away, but there was also another voice in his head, a much louder sinister one that was telling him to seize his opportunity. The man then satisfied his deprived sexual appetite on her rapidly cooling corpse.

When he had finished, he picked up a white plastic bag from his boot and wrapped the bloodied chopper in it, placed it back in the car before slowly closing the boot. Finally, he nonchalantly got into his car and slowly drove out of the wasteland and headed off into the night, leaving a scene of utter horror in his wake.

Year 1985

Part Two: The Real Bogeyman

Chapter 15
Emma Jackson

Emma Jackson was bathed in the mid-morning sunshine; she lay on her front and supported her head under her chin with her two chubby arms. Her face was heavily made up for a girl of her age. The blood red lipstick stood out like an ink stain on a white satin sheet because the rest of her face was deathly pale through a mixture of powder and foundation make-up. Sometimes, Boy George's white face and sharp eyebrows can really get out of hand. Emma was not naturally pale, but a rich caramel colour; her dad, whom she never met, was black and her mother was fair skinned.

As she lay on her bed, she squinted to see the washout ghostly images that moved on her loud illuminated television. 'If you have a problem, if no one else can help and if you can find them, then maybe you can hire the A-team.'

Not only did the bright light from her window fade her television screen, it also highlighted the numerous dust particles that leapt like ballerinas dancing across the stage, under their own spotlight beam.

Emma's bedroom was currently in the process of being decorated. To be honest, it was in the process of being decorated since the council moved her and her mother in when she was five that was over four years ago. Now her bedroom was decorated straight onto brownish red plaster with a faded, slightly damp 'My little Pony' poster that resembled vanilla Swiss rolls in the curled-up corners. She was definitely too old for 'My little pony' but hadn't bothered to replace it. Now Boy George was the one she loved. Her friends were all into that new girl Madonna, but not her. In fact, she was buzzing that day because there was a double page 'Culture Club' poster in the latest edition of 'Look-In' magazine. *I'll put that up later,* she thought.

"*Karma, karma karma karma karma chameleon, you come and go, you come and go,*" she sung to herself as she swayed her arms, pretending to be the flamboyant music star Boy George.

She'd asked her mum if they could get that new music channel MTV so she could watch his latest videos everyday not just wait for seven o'clock on Thursdays and hope that he was on 'Top of the Pops'. But Mum had said that they couldn't afford to get cable TV and reminded her that she was very lucky to have a TV in her room, because when she was a little girl they only had one TV in the house and it was only black and white. Why would people even bother to watch something that was always grey? *It sounded like the most boringness thing in the whole world,* she thought.

Her mother's voice woke her from daydream.

"Emma, Emma, go out you're spending too much time in your room, get some fresh air before supper," her mother shouted from the kitchenette down the corridor.

"Mum, I'm watching TV."

"No, not all day, get out and get some fresh air!" ordered her mum.

"Okay, I'll go and knock for Jenny," reluctantly, Emma shouted back.

Emma's mum, Crystal dried up the last of the pots and filled the kettle up and put it on the hob for a well-earned brew. She took down the blue and white sugar bowl which was adorned with faded Chinese figures crossing a bridge next to a circular fruit tree below a couple of swooping doves. Then she put two tea spoons of sugar into her pink 'World's best Mum' cup and dropped a square tea bag in, straight out of the 'Tetley' tea packet. The kettle gave a low whistle as it built up steam and covered the kitchenette in a fine steamy haze. The steam reminded her of the times she would be driving with Emma's dad. His car was always full of smoke, either cigarette but more often weed, especially if his teenage brothers tagged along for a joy ride.

A slight frown betrayed her feelings when she remembered the good times. Things were great with him at first, he would treat her like his princess surprising her with jewellery, perfume, spa treatments and fancy holidays, life was grand. However, life started going downhill rapidly when she started hinting that she wanted to take things further maybe by getting engaged. We don't have to set a date just get engaged so everyone knows that that you're off the market she joked. That was when she got her first crack. The second and third came when she suggested that he could see her more often, rather than giving the tarts that hung around the bowling green pub lifts everywhere. But all of the slaps and punches she received were like a playful tap compared to the beating when she told him that she was pregnant with his child. Her face was unrecognisable for months later. She even had a bruised 'L' shape on her cheek which could still be seen when the light caught it.

Fortunately, her baby was unharmed and she never saw Emma's father again. He had made his ideas on fatherhood abundantly clear. Crystal never mentioned his child to him ever again, she didn't even know if he knew if she had a boy or a girl. As far as he was concerned, both Crystal and her child never even existed.

Well, it appeared that a leopard doesn't change its spots; there was talk on the grapevine that he was doing time in Strangeways, finally they managed to pin something on him. The last thing she thought about before sitting down with her cuppa was, he should have been locked up for what he did to her years ago.

As Crystal enjoyed her brew, she could hear her daughter about to leave the house. Emma eventually got off her bed and turned off the dusty TV with BA Baracus shouting, 'Shut up, fool, I ain't gonna get on no plane' and pulled on her denim dungarees that were on top of the pile of clothing by her wardrobe. She put on her pink trainers and a red Boy George T-shirt and ran down the stairs shouting out, "Okay, Mum, I'll be home for supper." She closed the door to her upstairs flat 23A Erwood Drive in New Moston, North Manchester and walked to her friend Jenny's flat.

The hot early evening sun had turned everyone lazy; kids couldn't be bothered to run for the ice-cream van and couples sat in their front gardens sipping their 'Kestrel Pilsner's' lagers straight from the can. Some happy drunken lads dressed in red shirts spilled beer and sang loud football songs on the street corner.

Emma sauntered her way to the next street to knock on for Jenny and see if she wanted to go to the park for a few hours before it got dark. She knocked on Jenny's front door but her mother said that she was spending the weekend at her dad's and wouldn't be back until tomorrow.

A little disappointed, Emma said bye to Jen's mother and walked off to the corner shop. She had a one pound note in the pocket of her dungarees which should be enough money to buy a bottle of 'Happy Shopper Cola' and a posh half custard & strawberry lollipop and still have enough for a treat tomorrow. She purchased her treats from the new 7-eleven store which only opened last week but already she had visited three times. She drank her coke which fizzed and tickled her nose as she gulped it straight from the bottle. The gas made her burp which she followed by an 'excuse me' even though she was by herself it felt right to remember her manners. Emma licked her lollipop and did not pay any attention to the traffic on the street as she strolled across the road. She stepped out in front of a small black minivan and was shocked to hear the van screech to a halt when she was in the middle of the road.

Phew, it was a good job that the driver had been quick to react otherwise he might have knocked her over. The driver looked very kind, he didn't curse or swear at her using his fingers but just smiled. She waved to the him to thank him for stopping then did not pay any more attention to the black van or the vigilant driver as she ran the rest of the way to the park.

The lovely clear early summer's day slowly gathered a chill in the late afternoon air, as Emma started to rock herself on the black rubber seat of the swing. She had reached maximum height after only eight full swings and could now see over the rainbow coloured round-a-bout that still rotated with the momentum of its previous user. As she reached full height she saw a figure which got closer and closer. Although she had noticed the scruffy stranger as he approached her, she was still surprised when he stopped and asked her if she wanted a free pedigree pug puppy. He explained that he needed to get rid of some because he just couldn't sell them without their proper documentation.

Emma's eyes widen and her mouth opened before beaming into a smile. She was so excited because just the other day she had pestered her mum for ages for a puppy, but Mum had said that they were too expensive to buy and to look after. But now there was a chance to get one for free, Mummy would be so happy. That would save her hundreds of pounds and I bet that the money saved could be spent on dog food for the first few weeks. She could then use her pocket money to buy the rest and she won't ever moan or whine again about being bored because she'll have a dog to look after. Emma went with the man out of the park to where he said he had three puppies and that she could take her pick.

As they walked, Emma's excitement level was at ten. She couldn't wait to see, pet and play with the puppies. Her mind wandered as she started to think about names for her new pet, maybe Rainbow, Stardust or perhaps Mr T if it looked like a strong pup.

As they walked gradually a strange feeling came over her, she began to feel a little uneasy. Maybe it was that they had been walking down a remote alley and passed the deserted industrial estate where she could not see any other people. Perhaps it felt now that the stranger's hand was no longer holding her hand, but pulling her hand or even worse gripping her hand. Or maybe the words of her mother 'Don't ever go off with strangers 'began to resonate in her rapidly panicking brain.

"I've changed my mind, sir, we don't have room at home for a puppy," said Emma.

"It's okay, these dogs are only small they don't need much space," said the man.

"No, I don't think I will have the time to walk it every day," said Emma nervously.

Suddenly, she did her best to pull her hand from his calloused grip and make a run for it.

"That's okay, you can just let it out into your back garden to take a shit!" shouted the man.

With that he yanked her back and enclosed her with his sweaty arms under his black workman's coat in an effort to hide her away.

Emma screamed and tried to break free from the strange man gasp, she shouted for help but her screams were muffled by a rough, vile smelling hand. In desperation, she bit the fleshy part of his hand just below his fingers and kicked her legs because she couldn't move her arms at all, they were in a vice-like grip that continued to squeeze the breath out of her body. Suddenly, Emma felt a blow to the back of her head and the ground rushed up and hit the whole of her body with a dusty thud. At that same moment, someone turned off the sun and there was only darkness and silence.

Chapter 16
Old Man Fred

Barry Stone emptied the bubbling saucepan of baked beans onto the two slices of slightly overdone pieces of toast. The steaming bean sauce flooded the cream china plate as it soaked in, turning the toast red. He placed the plate alongside an orange squash in a small diamond-patterned glass tumbler and two white oval-shaped tablets onto a wooden tray. The exposed wooden floorboards creaked as he stepped on each one as he carried the tray upstairs. There was an unpleasant aroma in the air which only got stronger as he ascended the stairs. With some manoeuvring, he opened the door at the top of the stairs with his back. A black portable TV played and was on full blast. The football commentary got louder as he walked into the room. The air was heavy with ammonia like a public toilet with a broken flush. The dusty curtains were closed, even though it was sunny outside and a man in his late seventies lay on the bed, slightly propped up with a couple of off-white pillows. There were two suspicious milk bottles full of what looked like apple juice but definitely not milk. The man on the bed raised his arms towards the TV and gestured in frustration.

'Only ten minutes to go in the 1985 FA Cup final. The ball goes out to the right to Norman Whiteside who steps over the ball and shoots. Yes, he curled it past Southall to put United one-nil up' came the commentary from the TV.

"Oh, fucking hell, those fucking red twats have scored, how

the hell has he scored from there?" shouted the man lying on the bed.

"Oh, get in United... United! United!" cheered Barry.

"Oh, I forgot that you were a red... well, you say that you're a red but you're not even watching the cup final," said the man in the bed.

"Nah, you're right. I don't give a shit about football, just like winding you up," said Barry as he put the tray on a dusty dressing table next to an open bottle of 'Old Spice' and a plastic black comb with a clump of grey hair tangled in the teeth.

"It stinks of piss in 'ere, you dirty bastard Fred!"

"Sorry, Barry son, I couldn't make it to the toilet last night," said Fred

"Anyway, here's your tea," said Barry.

"What's this? Beans on fucking toast. I tell you what, Keith Floyd has got nothing to worry about with chefs like you," said Fred.

Barry sneered at Fred.

"Thanks, would be nice, you ungrateful shit! And are you thinking of getting dressed anytime soon and pissing off back to your own home so I can have my room back? My fucking back's killing me sleeping on that shitty sofa downstairs," Barry sniped back.

"Yeah, yeah, yeah. I told you when my foot's better, I'll be out of your hair," said Fred.

"You fell off your ladder three weeks ago and even then, the doctor said it was just a sprain! I've had enough, I want you out tomorrow you can go hop around your own hovel," said Barry.

"Where's your respect for your step father?" said Fred.

"You aren't my step father, you're just someone Mum's shacked up with, so I want you gone in the morning," said Barry.

"I don't know, Barry son, I quite like living here with you and I don't think you have much of a choice." A wry smile spread across Fred's face.

"You see, son, the other day I went to your shed to get my buckets back and I found a bin bag with some very strange things in it," said Fred.

Barry was about to leave the room when he stopped dead in his tracks.

"Why is it a fifty-seven-year-old man has a bin bag full of little girls' clothes and things. Dresses, dungarees and a half pack of Happy Families. I'm sure that detective that came asking questions about the Fry girl would find it more than interesting," said Fred.

Barry's fists clenched as the vein pulsed in his forehead, but a voice at the back of his head said 'he will keep, he will keep'. Fred then held out his hand with a crumbled up fiver in it.

"Bazza son, could you put a fiver on the nose for 'Forgive & Forget' at five thirty at Goodwood."

Barry slowly took the fiver without even looking at Fred as he held onto the fiver for a moment longer just as the phone rang downstairs.

"Don't forget the horse now, son, forgive & forget," said Fred.

Barry walked downstairs at a snail's pace because the phone had already stopped ringing so there was no point rushing. He checked his answer phone just as Fred started again cursing at the TV as the final whistle neared.

A high pitch beep sounded before the recorded message came through:

Hello, Mr Stone, I need someone to come over and clear the leaves that have gathered in my conservatory gutter. It's blocking the rainwater, please come around this afternoon between 5 and 6. My name is Ruby Dunne and the address is 11 Talbot Drive, New Moston.

The message ended and Barry put down the receiver and thought maybe he should get rid of the bin bag from the shed. But then a better idea came to his head, maybe he should have a real clear out. He wouldn't need the duct tape or cable ties from the van, just a special ingredient that would enhance his guest's culinary experience. He jotted down the woman's address on a Post-it note pad kept by the phone as he thought he must stop at 'Patel's News' corner shop for some more cans of Special Brew, there may be a celebration soon.

Chapter 17
Barry Stone

Barry shrugged as he picked up his tool bag and scratched his unkempt bearded chin which merged into the wispy strands on the side of his balding head. He left his mid terrace house and put his tools in the back of his black minivan, whose interior could not be seen from the road because the van doors did not have windows. Inside the van were all sorts of equipment any self-respecting handy-man should always have; various types of tapes, Sellotape, masking tape, strong duct tape, an assortment of ropes and cable ties. A rusty foldaway ladder and a myriad of screws, nuts, bolts and whatever else is hidden away under all the bric-a-brac. There was one object that didn't quite belong with the other stuff and that was a dark green dusty tartan blanket with tassels at the ends.

Barry flopped into his smoky, stale-smelling van and started on the twenty-minute drive to New Moston. His eyes were constantly on the lookout for any opportunities that may come his way. He saw a girl sauntering slowly with a football under her arm while licking a rapidly melting ice cream, but no good because ten yards behind were her parents also licking their 99s.

Then he saw a chubby girl come out of the 7-eleven corner shop. She opened a bottle of cola and slurped down the black liquid as it fizzed over the plastic rim and the bubbles made her cough. He diligently watched her and his gaze never left, as she strolled down the street. He hadn't had this feeling since last year in Shaw, behind the High Street and the girl with red hair. The girl took another sip of her drink and stepped out onto the road. He had plenty of time to brake but sped up slightly just to jam on his brakes. So, it appeared that he was a very conscientious driver. But little did the girl know that he was watching her like a hawk.

He parked his black minivan and began to prowl on foot. He saw the girl walk towards the swings in the playground section of the park. None of the other children seemed to take notice of him in his working coat and shabby overalls as he strode across the expanse of an open field. They were too intent on playing football with jumpers for goal post, running and playing catch, running on the tunnels and swinging from the monkey bars.

He approached with his old familiar lines; he knew that nothing got the child's attention like getting something for free especially if that something was a cute pedigree puppy.

He approached the girl and said, "I don't suppose you want a free pedigree pug by any chance?" The girl's face lit up and her brightening mood was mirrored in the face of Barry as a slight sneer curled in the corner of his mouth.

"Come on and take your pick, otherwise someone else will have them if you don't come now," said Barry.

He held her hand and led her out of the park towards his small black minivan. She was carefree and excited about meeting the puppies but as they entered the deserted industrial estate behind the park, he could feel a change of tone in the girl's voice. There was a quiver that had developed and that she was trying her hardest to hide and act calm. He could also feel her hand start to wriggle and try to work its way free from his. He had done his best to sweet-talk the girl until he finally ran out of patience when she tried to run from him.

Alarm bells went off in his head and he knew she must be silenced. He pulled her close and tried to smother her cries. The little bitch fucking bit his hand and was trying to kick the shit out of him. Barry thought he needed to shut her up, so reached into his pocket and smacked her on the back of the head with his large iron spanner that he always kept in his inside jacket pocket and knocked her unconscious. By smacking her with all of his strength, he lost his grip of her and she fell flat onto the dusty ground.

Shit! shit! Quick, into the van, out of sight before anyone sees. He bundled her into the back of his van and covered her unconscious body with the dark green tartan blanket which he kept for such an occasion. He then got into his van and drove off without anyone reacting to the girl's body thudding on the ground, her brief cry for help or her being bundled into the van. The smoke from the van's exhaust as it sped off and the dust cloud kicked up by the tyres lingered for the briefest moment in the air on that hazy summer's day. Unlike the black van, which made a sharp left turn up a side street and then was gone from view with its chugging engine fading into the distance.

Chapter 18
Nick Ross

Barry Stone opened up the tightly sealed plastic bag which was wedged tight in the cupboard under the sink between a container of white bleach and a can of red Mr Sheen furniture polish. He spread the couple of days out-of-date copy of 'The Mirror' newspaper on his beige kitchen surface. The headline read 'Live Aid Rocked with Love' with an energetic Mick Jagger and Tina Turner prancing on stage. Carefully, he took out the yellow packet within the bag which contained mostly oriental writing with a large white sticker that was hand-stuck to the side of it. The sticker had a large skull and cross-bones motif similar to that on a pirate ship and large bold letters which spelled out 'Poison Arsenic'.

With great care, he filled a single tea-spoon from the packet and began to stir it into the grey chicken and sweet corn soup that was simmering on the hob. The chicken soup mixed with potent burning smell of the Arsenic was powerful enough to singe your nasal hairs, if inhaled too deeply. *I'm sure Fred is going to enjoy his supper with the special ingredient. That will teach him to try and blackmail me,* thought Barry as the grey powder slowly dissolved without a trace.

As he took the bowl of soup and slice of stiffening bread up the rickety stairs, the evening news had just finished and the continuity announcer could be heard from the TV downstairs. 'Here on BBC One is your chance to help the police identify wanted criminals with Nick Ross and Sue Cook, it is Crimewatch UK'. A snare drum and electronic keyboard cut into the silence over the backdrop of a rotating blue siren.

After he dropped off Fred's supper, Barry came down and settled down on the sofa with a can of celebration 'Special Brew'. The program had been on for half an hour or so before it grabbed his attention when the police inspector and the presenter Nick Ross were in mid conversation.

"... Three hours later when Emma failed to return home, the police were called and a full-scale search was started," said Inspector Rudd.

"I understand that the missing person's investigation soon turned into a murder inquiry less than two weeks later," said Nick Ross.

"Yes, Nick, the missing person investigation was upgraded to a murder investigation when the body of a nine-year-old girl was found on wasteland by a lady walking her dog. Emma had been sexually assaulted and strangled; I personally had to break that devastating news to her mother. I hope and pray that I never have to do that again due to the actions of this man. So, please, could your viewers ring in if they remember anything no matter how insignificant they think it is," said Inspector Rudd.

"Thank you, Inspector Rudd, we now have a reconstruction of the day, in question," said Nick.

The reconstruction started with a voice over of film footage of Erwood Drive the road in New Moston where Emma walked down to knock for her friend and the park where she was last seen. The reconstruction ended with footage of a middle-aged woman walking her brown and white border collie and discovering the dead girl's body in a patch of stinging nettles. Over the dogs barking, the woman could be heard saying, "Easy girl, heel."

"I understand that some of the children who were in the park were able to give you a photo fit," said Nick as the camera panned back on him.

"Yes, Nick, we have a photo fit of a person of interest that was seen talking to Emma and we would like to eliminate him from our enquiries. He is described as being in his late sixties..."

Barry spat out his mouthful of bitter special brew. "For fuck's sake, those cheeky shits, no way do I look like I'm in my late sixties! Anyone over forty might as well be in the hundreds according to those shits."

Inspector Rudd continued with his description, "He was wearing dirty overalls like he worked in the manual trade like a plumber or mechanic and he wore a dark blue work jacket which the children described as a bin man's jacket."

Fucking hell, that's another bloody jacket I'm going to have to dump, he thought.

"Could you tell us about the clothing that she was wearing, I understand it is very distinctive," said Nick.

"Yes, Emma was last seen wearing a bright red t-shirt with an image of the pop star Boy George on the front. I understand that these t-shirts are extremely rare, so if you have been sold one or come across one, it would be of great interest to us."

"Thank you, Inspector Rudd. Let's hope that the reconstruction jogs someone's memory. Don't forget it was a sweltering day, Saturday, 18th May, the same day Manchester United won the FA Cup final at Wembley."

The camera slowly panned across the studio as Nick walked over to join his co-host.

"That is all we have time for in this the main program. Please join us in one hour for Crimewatch UK update, but if you are

116

unable to please remember that you are still highly unlikely to be the victim of serious crime, so please do sleep well, don't have nightmares. Goodnight," said Nick.

The co-presenter Sue Cook's massive ruby ring sparkled as she waved her papers and said goodnight just as the drums and electronic music was heard again. The music from the TV could not quite drown out the sounds of spluttering, groaning and coughing coming from the bedroom at the top of the stairs.

Chapter 19
The White Hart

Barry's selfish attitude told him he needed to protect the only person he cared about; himself. He had better lie low for a while because at that moment he was taking too many risks and the more risks the more chance of exposure and capture. In other words, the more remote the better; less people meant less chance of being recognised. So, he was more than pleased to be out of the big city of Manchester and had taken a job, clearing a house for the recently deceased Ex-University Lecturer Professor Rizwan. The work was hard especially with the biting cold and blizzard conditions affecting this part of rural Huddersfield. Even though this area was miles out of his usual work radius, his motto was that 'he went where the work was'; North Yorkshire, Failsworth, Shaw, and New Moston plus the hirer, Professor Rizwan's son's desperation doubled his usual daily fee. No sane person would work when everything else was closed, especially three days before Christmas. All train journeys were cancelled; several power lines and telephone lines were brought down by the previous night's blizzard. Communication, difficult at the best of times, was now nearly impossible.

After finishing up the last of his manual slog, Barry started the hazardous drive back to Greater Manchester. There were a few cars that had braved the conditions post blizzard. But they had slipped and spun uncontrollably across the almost deserted country lanes, and now lay abandon like toy cars left out after play against the glistening white moorland. He thought maybe this wasn't the best idea, to be out on these treacherous roads as he drove through the West Yorkshire town of Marsden.

He had been travelling at barely over fifteen miles an hour when his van started the prolonged climb up the barren country road and his only thought was to get back home and get some much-needed shut eye. The welcoming sight of a country pub didn't even prick his attention, a cold pint, a hot meal or even an uncomfortably full bladder did not interest him. Nothing was going to make him break his drive home. Well almost nothing, he wasn't planning to see the only thing that would make him stop his van; an unaccompanied girl. There she was sliding down a snow-covered slide, playing with her pink doll. She had kicked the layers of snow into one huge mound. Sending her doll down the slide then followed her down with a squeal and a crunch into the compacted snow. Slowly, the virgin snow was being polluted and it had turned into the dirty muddy slush. Nevertheless, the girl let out yells of excitement as she descended again and again down the glistening slide.

He parked his car by the 'The White Hart' public house carpark which was deserted apart from a car that was buried under the snow, and would have taken ten men ten hours to dig it out. The small hill just about resembled a car shape. Barry knew that this was potentially the only working car that he could see. So, he knew if he got away, there would be no catching him.

The warm air was certainly welcomed as Barry entered the almost empty pub and sat down on a stool near the bar underneath a giant Christmas tree dripping with silver baubles. From his position, he could see all the occupants of the bar area which was smothered with shiny plastic purple and pink linked angel decorations. He could also see the small pub playground through the white stencilled snowman on the window. Apart from the elderly man who was serving behind the wooden bar and an equally elderly lady wiping tables, and spreading out cardboard coasters, the vast bar area only had two more people. They were two men drinking coffee and chatting. One of the men wore a red insulated walking jacket and the other had on a green walking jacket. The man who wore the red jacket face seemed strangely familiar to Barry, but he couldn't think where or when he had seen him before. Underneath their table lay two bulging rucksacks together with a smaller pink rucksack. One of the men kept an eye on the girl playing outside, while the other held a newspaper on his lap. Both men were just out of ear shot of him so he couldn't quite hear what they were talking about, just caught the occasional word. 'Thousand pounds' and 'Crimewatch'.

The Landlord approached Barry from behind the bar and asked him what he fancied.

"Afternoon, could I have a small Guinness," responded Barry

"Comin' right up, sir," replied the barman in a cheery tone.

As Barry sipped the white creamy head of his drink, he watched as one of the men stood up and walked out of the bar area towards the toilets. While the other man had a quick glance out of the window at the girl playing then started reading the 'News of The World' newspaper. As the man became enthralled in what he was reading, he saw his chance. He slipped out of the pub and shuffled briskly towards the girl. There was no disarming patter, no coercion, just straight to abduction. She didn't have a chance to scream as the spanner connected with the back of her head. The sound of her body falling to the ground was muffled by the snow-covered ground. Without looking around to see if he had been spotted, he quickly pulled the girl's unconscious body into the back of his small minivan and threw the dark green tartan blanket over her.

Barry's heart almost beat out of his chest as he rushed to get into his van to make his escape, when the man from the bar wearing the red jacket intercepted him as Barry opened the driver's door. The man's face was full of rage and panic as he pummelled him with punches to the stomach and bent him double. Barry managed to get up but then was smashed in the face by the man's right hand which broke his nose as blood squirted everywhere all over the man's red walking jacket and himself. The man was still so full of rage that he brought his fist back for another right-hand punch to the face when Barry pulled out his trusted iron spanner from inside his jacket pocket and swung it towards the man's face; he caught him square on his left temple. The blow was enough to send the man back with an initial stumble then he collapsed in a heap on the snow, covered with Barry's blood and now his own bloody head-wound.

A weary, heavily breathing Barry stumbled and held onto the side of his van to steady his legs. His chest visible rose as he wheezed to get more oxygen into his lungs. He fumbled with the car door with a growing sense of panic and urgency and started the engine. Before he had a chance to set off, he saw the other man in the green jacket from the pub come hurtling down the path towards him. *First gear and get out of here,* he thought. The man in the green jacket blocked his path and approached at speed, waving his arms and shouting for assistance. There was only one choice for Barry; to knock him out of the way. The only thought he kept telling himself was 'he couldn't be caught if he didn't stop' so he floored the van and crashed straight into the approaching man's right leg and sent him hurtling into the air and came down with a crash into the piled-up snow on the side of the lane.

As Barry sped off up the snowy incline, he saw the man that he knocked over still in a heap in the snow, but there was movement in the man in the red jacket that he had knocked out with his spanner. He saw the man groggily get to his feet as the van approached an upcoming bend and then disappeared from his rear-view mirror as it entered a forest lane. He drove his dent-ridden minivan fast up the long winding road. His previous concern for the icy conditions had been superseded by his panic to get away. He cursed his bloody nose while at the same time counting his lucky stars that he managed to get away from the two men. As the road snaked back out of the forest in his rear-view mirror, he could see that the landlord and landlady were now outside the pub helping the two men that he had left on the ground.

The metallic tang of blood was pungent on Barry's tongue as he grabbed a grey oily rag to stem the blood flow from his busted nose. Indeed, after two minutes of constant pressure, the blood stopped pouring.

That bloody bastard has broken my bloody nose so he got what he deserved. I suppose a busted-up nose is a small price to pay when escaping with my prize. Try and catch me in this weather with no vehicle. Ha! They will never be able to catch up with me now. By the time the cops turn up, I'll be miles away and good luck running my stolen number plates that won't get them very far, Barry thought as his black van struggled up the skiddy forest hill road, leaving a trail of smoke and exhaust fumes.

The sun shone low through the forest trees and blinded him for a second as he pulled the driver's visor down to block out the sharp glare. All he could think of was putting more distance between himself and any possible pursuers. A slight sneer lifted the right side of his mouth as he thought that even if they could get up here in time a police helicopter would struggle to locate him in the thick wooded lanes almost completely covered by the enormous established pine trees.

After he drove flat out for two hours straight, Barry finally pulled off the winding country lane and drove deep into a woodland path. The sign ahead told him that he just entered the grounds of Fountains Abbey and he could see the ancient ruins silhouetted against the murky late-evening sky. He found a secluded spot as he stopped the van and breathed a massive sigh of relief. A twist of the ignition key allowed the struggling engine to finally rest. A flick of the headlight switch left the van in complete darkness. There wasn't even the soft light of the moon to break through the gloom.

Barry's once racing heart-beat had now returned to something like normal. His bloody nose had dried into his now matted beard. His breathing too had returned to normal now since the drama of his escape. But now his excitement level began to rise once again when he thought about his prize. Now he sat in complete silence even his tools had ceased to rattle surrounded by the deathly quiet that was a great relief to him. The blackness and the thick forest was a safety blanket that engulfed him and gave him the secrecy he desired. He opened his glove compartment and popped in a breath freshener as he walked around to open the van's rear doors. There was loud squeak as he opened the first door. And just at that moment the stillness of the late evening woodland was completely shattered by a blood curdling scream, a scream of pure terror.

Chapter 20
Jessica Rudd

The gentle snow slowly descended like wedding confetti caught on the breeze, as Clayton woke up early on that winter's morning. It was late December, only three days before Christmas. Why he had to sleep at a B&B was beyond him as he only lived forty minutes down the road. But Hannah and Jess had said it is more like a holiday when you wake up somewhere new. Well at least it was mid-Luna cycle with fourteen days until the next full moon, so staying at a B&B wasn't really a major problem. He knew he had to get up early and was looking forward to today like the proverbial hole in the head. Secretly, he had hoped that the whole walking weekend thing would be called off due to the horrendous blizzard the previous day. But Jessica had pleaded to keep the weekend away with Mum and Dad and, of course, Michael had to come too. To say things were a little strange between them was an understatement. Yes, they are work colleagues but were never good friends, so when he started dating and then married Hannah, things got a little awkward around the police station. It is fine to say to someone's face that 'no, they didn't mind that they are dating your ex' but when it happens you can never truly be one hundred per cent okay with the idea'.

Clayton, Michael, Hannah and Jessica set off for their walking weekend to a remote part of Huddersfield near the town of Marsden. They were not going to let the snow scupper their plans. Jess had said that the snow was going to add to the excitement 'it will be like walking in a Winter Wonderland' and besides there was no such thing as bad weather, only inappropriate clothing.' She imparted her words of wisdom while she threw her pink cabbage patch doll 'Molly' into the air and caught it. Clayton pulled on his red insulated jacket and packed the last of his camping gear into his already stuffed rucksack. In the hallway of the almost deserted Bed & Breakfast, he met up with Jessica and her step-father Michael Baker.

"Where's Hannah?" Clayton asked.

"She says that she will have to give today's walk around a miss. She thinks she's twisted her ankle when we were walking through that god-awful blizzard last night," said Michael.

"Oh, great it was her who insisted on this walking weekend and she is the first one missing in action," Clayton remarked.

Clayton thought that this was going to be a long and awkward day walking if he had to chat with Michael. At least Hannah could have acted as a go between them, peacemaker and break any awkward silences. Maybe this was her way of getting them to say more than two words to each other. After all, one was Jessica's dad and the other her step-dad.

They decided to walk though Marsden Moor which was a very steep climb especially carrying their supplies in their backpacks, but the views were simply breath-taking with the snow settled all around on the tree tops and hills as far as the eye could see.

After trekking for two hours, they came across a more than welcome sight; a remote pub called the 'The White Hart'. It stood out against the bleak snowy moorland and a frozen reservoir opposite both of which were separated by a deserted country lane that headed up to the hillside forest.

"Look you two a pub who fancies a drink," said Clayton as

he pointed to the building in the distance.

"Sounds good to me," said Michael.

They made their way to the entrance and shook off the light dusting of snowflakes from their jackets.

Both Clayton and Michael order a large coffee and they got a hot chocolate with marshmallows and cream for Jessica.

"Michael, can I go out and play on the slide for a bit," asked Jessica.

An awkward silence instantly descended on the party.

"I think you had better ask your dad, Jess," said Michael.

"Yes, it's okay. You go and play, thanks for asking, make sure you stay by the slide, Monkey Nut!" said Clayton

Jess gave her dad a hug and taking her cabbage patch doll 'Molly' ran out to play on the slide and the snow.

As Jess went out to play, Clayton and Michael sat down at a table and sipped their steaming cups of coffee. On the table was a complimentary issue of 'The News of the World' newspaper which Michael causally picked up and thumbed through. The FrontPage headline read '£1,000 for the capture of the Bogeyman.'

Just at the moment, a shabby man walked into the pub and sat down underneath the large Christmas tree perched on the bar. He wore grey jogging bottoms that were splattered with a combination of paint, plaster and who knows what else. He wore a heavy-looking leather jacket with the collar turned up, obscuring the lower half of his face and sat on a stool at the bar to order a drink.

"Whose idea was the reward?" asked Michael.

"The paper approached Hannah and she thought £1,000 would definitely sharpen people's minds if nothing else. He may get shopped by his nearest and dearest. Maybe Sonia might have taken the reward money and dobbed in Peter if there was £1,000 on the line." Both men laughed at Clayton's dry joke and took a sip of their coffee.

"Anyway, I'm doing another Crimewatch appeal next month. Hopefully, we get some more witnesses," said Clayton

Both men sat at the table and enjoyed their warming coffee while Jessica played in the snowy playground attached to the rear of the pub.

Clayton said as he stood up from the table, "I'm just going to the toilet for a second, keep an eye on Jess, will you?"

Michael nodded and had a look out of the window then glanced back down to the newspaper on his lap. He flicked through it and glanced at various articles that didn't really catch his attention 'Chart toppers Queen banned in America', 'Sinclair C5 hits the road' and 'Another body of a woman found in Burnley' Michael continued to read until Clayton came back to the table shaking his hands.

"Bloody hand dryer not working," he said.

"Oh, it's not the five-star services you're used to," responded Michael with a teasing tone.

Clayton smiled and walked over to the large window that looked out onto the playground.

"Where's Jess?" he asked.

"She should be outside, not unless she's gone round the front," responded Michael.

An awful sinking feeling pulled at Clayton's stomach.

"Okay, you go out the front and check, I'll go to the playground," said Clayton.

Clayton briskly walked to the front of the pub and saw something that chilled him to the bone. Jess' doll lay in the snow with a massive boot print on its head. Then he saw a sight that almost stopped his heart, the shabby man who was sitting in the pub a moment ago was putting a floppy, unconscious Jess in the back of his small minivan. His blood boiled as he sprinted over to the man and unleashed all of his rage on him. He caught him about to get into the driver's seat of the van. Adrenaline mixed with fear powered Clayton's blows as he connected with the man's face. One punch two punch and the third punch broke the man's nose as there was an explosion of crimson blood splattered over his jacket. The injury to the man didn't stop Clayton's anger as he again went to punch the man straight on the face then a large iron spanner came from his blind-side and cracked him on the side of the head. He lost all feeling as his world turned into a blur, his legs felt unsteady and then nothing as they both buckled and he fell on the slushy snow underneath his boots.

Michael heard the commotion while looking for Jess at the front of the pub, he saw the man strike Clayton with the spanner as he sprinted towards them. He saw the man jump into his van and wheel spin up the road towards him. Michael thought the only way of stopping the van was to stand in the road and try to block his escape route. But the speeding van did not slow down at all; if anything, it sped up. The tyres slid across the icy lane as its engines squealed like a rat caught in a trap. The oncoming van was like an onrushing bull and this particular matador lost his nerve. Michael thought it was not going to stop and at the very last second tried to avoid the speeding vehicle with a quick jump out of the way. But the van driver swerved intentionally towards him and crunched his right knee with his bumper, shattering Michael's knee cap and sending him flying through the air and thudding onto the piled-up snow on the side of the road. Part of his bone protruded from out of his walking pants as he screamed from the pain. He was going into shock and was slipping in and out of consciousness. The landlady who saw the carnage taking place came running out. She held one hand over her mouth and the other held her flapping coat closed as she bent down to comfort Michael.

"Don't move, Derek, my husband is ringing for an ambulance and the police."

Her attention was then drawn to the comatose bloody body of Clayton. As she ran over to him, she saw him slowly lift himself from the snow and gingerly touched the side of his head, which had stopped bleeding but seemed to have swollen to the size of an ostrich egg. The distraught landlady approached him and said, "Sit down, son, you have a massive swelling, you may have a concussion, the police are on their way."

Her words didn't even register in Clayton's brain. He opened his eyes still dazed from the blow but soon this was replaced by alarm; he realised that there were no other vehicles close by and he was stuck. The pure agony of Jess being abducted was tearing him apart. He felt helpless; fear and pain were welling up in him. He knew that being such a remote location the police response could take up to an hour and the perpetrator might be miles away by then. The only thought was to save his daughter and he would do anything. Instinctively he ran up the lane in a vain attempt to catch up with the skidding minivan and cursed aloud as he saw the smoke and fumes chug out from the exhaust pipe as it strained up the sharp winding incline and disappeared behind the emerging forest. Clayton ran after the van, unwilling to give up in his hopeless pursuit, tears flooded his eyes and stung him as he ran on against the biting wind sweeping down from the freezing hills. He ran and ran in a vain attempt to catch up the van until his body could not trudge any longer through the now knee-high snow. Suddenly, a shooting pain exploded in his left leg as his Achilles tendon snapped under the constant stress. His running then became a desperate hobble as he gasped for breath and eventually his body gave up and he collapsed in the snow from a mixture of exhaustion and agony. His body fell and slid down a steep embankment until it crashed on the frozen surface of canal just at the entrance to a long black tunnel. The crash of his body on the hard ice broke a rib and left him winded and motionless as a dusting of snow began to settle on top of him along with disturbed snow that cascaded down from the canal's edge and slowly enveloped him.

As he lay in the freezing snow, his body battered from a combination of the two-mile sprint, the aching in his side and the swelling to the side of his head making him increasingly groggy. The now sub-zero temperature was quickly cooling his overworked muscles and soon he experienced frostbite from the snow on his exposed face and hands. The onset of hyperthermia slowly took hold as he lay motionless, face-down, dying on the frozen canal covered in the biting snow.

Chapter 21
Daddy

Close contact with freezing snow initially feels like it is burning the skin so horrible is the pain. But soon the pain goes when the numbness sets in. The nerve endings become so cold that they lose their ability to transfer pain. All thoughts slowly die away too as the darkness in the brain begins to grow. Clayton could feel the numbness seep into him and numbness brings death. Slowly all of his internal organs were starting to fail, his blood pressure had plummeted. His face that was most exposed had suffered severe frost bite and both eyes were now frozen shut.

Certain death was only a moment away, no sound could he make, no movement. Only one thought went through his head, just the one thought as his head was slowly covered in more freshly disturbed snow. Ten years ago, when he made his oath to serve the public as a Police constable he never once questioned it but something was tearing him up inside. Yes, he was a policeman and now an inspector and he swore to uphold the law, and he had always believed in the judicial system. Yes, he was a policeman but above everything else in his life even his commitment to his chosen vocation, even above being a person. He was something far more valuable. He was a father. There was someone that called him 'Daddy' and that someone, Jessica, was now in mortal danger and she was now his one priority.

Clayton had always been a law-abiding citizen but laws and morals were things that he could not consider at this particular time. Hate filled up in him, the want to murder the man that had taken his daughter had completely overtaken him. All he wanted to do is to save his daughter, protect her by whatever means possible. He wanted so badly to catch the man in the van, hurt him with his bare fist and keep attacking him until he was no longer a threat to his Jess. Yes, he wanted to kill the man with all of his being that was the only thing that was going through his head, to kill him, kill him, kill him!

A werewolf was always summoned by his mistress the moon and must always change when it is highest in the sky. But what a lot of people don't know is that a werewolf can break out at any time if the host becomes wholly obsessed with killing and is filled with an absolute murderous intent and a longing for blood. It will break out of the host and seek out blood.

Clayton's world had come crashing down, that death was beginning to be seen as a sweet release. Buried in the snow and with the last drop of energy left in his body and his final breaths he screamed Jess! Jess! No! The word 'no' became a strangulated howl as his face twisted and fangs forced through from his gums. Jet black hairs spouted from every pore of his body as his bones crack and reform into an eight feet tall raging beast of a werewolf. One claw cracked through the ice as it stepped up onto the canal edge and ripped off the ragged torn-up jacket that hung loose around his neck. It sniffed the wet blood that was splashed all along the collar and dripped down the zip. He stiffed as he tasted the blood and howled in anticipation for now he had a taste for blood, so the hunt was on.

Immediately, the werewolf leapt and sprinted, trying to catch up with the van. Now that the werewolf had the taste of the man's blood on its tongue there was no escape, for it could smell the slightest fragrance on the breeze or taste the minute drop of his sweat in the air. As the beast bounded through the snow-covered woods and boggy swamps, he picked up other scents in the air, an elderly couple walking, the far-off camping site full of beavers and scouts. But the only thing on his mind was tracking down and killing the man that abducted his daughter and saving her life.

The werewolf ran constantly for hour after hour dodging trees in the forest that border the country road, leaping over walls, bounding over roads, diving through tunnels doing everything he could to keep the scent of the man in his nose. Eventually, the van pulled off the main winding lane onto something resembling a dirty track with a ruin of an abbey in the distance and finally stopped. The black van's exhaust spat out a final chug of grey smoke as the engine fell silent. In the distance the beast saw the man step out of the driver's door and strode to the back of the van and twisted the metal handle. With a squeak he pulled open the door and just before he had a chance to open the second door the Werewolf leapt through the air and with one muscular claw gripped the man by the top of his head. Each claw ripped into Barry's skull and produced a single line of blood that dripped down his head and onto his dark blue jacket. He screamed a blood curdling scream as the werewolf slowly twisted its giant claw and stared with its yellow eyes right into the man's face. It snarled with hatred, pure hatred for the man. With a speed and force that Barry couldn't see or indeed comprehend, the werewolf stuck his other claw straight through his bloody neck and dragged his claw straight down. Shredding his body into tattered ribbons and separated his head from his body. The beast then tossed the pulping mess of what was left of his body into the woods to its right and then hurled the still blinking head to the left deep into the undergrowth in the shadow of the ruined abbey.

There was a moan from inside the van as Jessica turned in her slumber, the effects of the blow to her head slowly beginning to wear off. At this point the werewolf leapt into the air back the way he had come; in the distance there was a faint howl carried on the wind.

Chapter 22
Dr Chen

The werewolf ran back through the forest, muddy swamps and over the same fields. Passed abandoned farmhouses until he reached the spot where a few hours earlier Clayton Rudd had become a bloodthirsty beast. There wasn't a moon to dictate the time when the beast should be silent and the man should return. So, although it was still pitch black the beast's claws slowly retracted away back into fingertips. His muzzle gradually melted away back into Clayton's nose and face. It lost a significant amount of height as its legs shortened and lost its black furry covering and bent back into the shape of a human leg. After two minutes of metamorphosis, Clayton was standing in the same spot where he had become the werewolf more than five hours previously. The changed had fixed his previous aliments, no longer did he have a bruised head; a torn Achilles tendon and his broken rib were now fully healed. Around his waist, he still wore his shredded grey walking pants but the rest of his clothing was nowhere to be seen. He didn't have any time to consider the situation he was in because head lights of a police car came closer up the frosty country lane.

The blue lights of the police Rover car reflected off the snow-covered fields. It skidded slightly on the country road before stopping and two police officers disembarked, holding torches with beams that sparkled the icy lane. The first officer to reach him was female, a tall blonde-haired policewoman WPC

Megson. She made some communication into her radio that Clayton couldn't quite hear. As she walked over to him, she started to unfold a tin foil style blanket and wrapped it around his bare shoulders.

"Inspector Rudd, thank goodness you're okay, we were dispatched over four hours ago when your daughter was reported as abducted. I have brilliant news for you, sir. We have just got word from North Yorkshire constabulary that they have picked her up. She has been taken to the St James Hospital in Leeds with a slight concussion," said WPC Megson.

The news that his daughter was safe affected Clayton and he dropped to his knees and held his head in his hands. The other police officer crouched down and helped Clayton stand up and helped him into the warmth of the back of the police car.

"Good evening, sir. I'm PC Makinson, can I just ask you what happened have you been attacked? Where are all your clothes."

"Leave it, Mackie, he's in shock," said WPC Megson.

"Thanks, yes. I'll rather just rest for a minute or two," said Clayton.

He sat back in the back seat of the police car as it drove slowly on the slippery country lane past the White Hart Pub that still had a police car parked outside with a section of the road cordoned off with blue and white police tape. During the journey, he nodded off for a half an hour through a combination of exhaustion and the warm police car. The brief sleep was halted as the car jerked as it rounded a corner.

WPC Megson noticed that he was waking up from his slumber as she began to talk to him.

"It's really good to see you, sir. To be honest, we had serious doubts that we would find you alive with these weather conditions and the injury you sustained. The previous shift had a panda car up here searching for you for an hour, so we didn't have much hope when we came on shift."

"So, when you saw me you had a pretty good idea that you found me, unless there was another thirty-year-old Caucasian wondering around up here," sarcastically joked Clayton.

"I knew it was you, sir. I recognised your face, I attended your training course on ethics and the police force when I was a police cadet," said WPC Megson.

"Thank you, sorry. I didn't recognise you."

"Well, I was one of fifty odd, I won't hold it against you," teased WPC Megson.

They continued for a few minutes in silence until Clayton asked, "Where are we heading, WPC Megson?"

"We are going to Saint Francis of Assisi General Hospital in Huddersfield to have you checked out. It's only another five minutes. It's the same hospital where they took your friend Michael Baker," replied WPC Megson.

"Why, what happened to Michael?" asked Clayton.

"It appears he was struck by your assailant's car when fleeing the scene."

As the car continued, Clayton just stared out of the window at the fluttering snowflakes illuminated by the flashing blue light, he must have dosed off again because the next thing he knew he was being taken to the hospital in a wheelchair and placed on a stretcher and taken to a female doctor who seemed to have Chinese heritage, where he was given a full medical examination. The doctor was in her late twenties and looked surprisingly young to be qualified. She introduced herself as Dr Victoria Chen specialist Trauma consultant

"It is remarkable, Inspector Rudd, but all of your vital signs are excellent. You are in brilliant health. We had a report that you were attacked by a heavy-duty spanner which knocked you unconscious. Your left temple doesn't show any signs of any recent trauma. There isn't any swelling or even a scratch on your head," said Dr Chen.

"Maybe he didn't catch me a good as it seemed," said Clayton.

"But he did catch you well enough to knock you unconscious, Inspector Rudd," said Dr Chen.

"I guess so," he said.

"You are also very lucky to be out on a night like this and not be suffering from extreme hyperthermia especially when you are not dressed appropriately. Inspector, my suggestion is that we monitor you for the next eight hours or so just to ensure that there are no latent effects of hyperthermia that haven't manifested themselves yet," said Dr Chen.

He wasn't really in a position to argue with the medical professionals and just let them do their tests, so he agreed to move to a private room for the rest of the night. Twenty minutes later, Clayton was on the hospital bed in his private room with a multitude of wires measuring his heart rate, blood pressure and monitoring his body temperature, he was also inhaling pure oxygen following medical protocol. Laying in the virtual darkness, his eyes began to feel heavy but sleep did not come in the hour or so since the doctor had left him. Eventually his eyes did start to close but just then, there was a voice behind his bed curtain.

"Clayton, Clayton, are you awake?" asked Hannah.

"Oh, hi, Hannah, yes, yes, I'm still awake," replied Clayton.

Hannah hobbled and winced up to the bed and instinctively hugged Clayton as they embraced, both started to bawl and shake

138

as their emotions finally came out. They wiped their eyes before Hannah pulled up a blue plastic chair to the bed and sat down padding her eyes with a 'Handy Andies' tissue and popped the packet back into her black leather purse.

"Jess is being brought here by ambulance once they check her out at Saint James. From what they have told me, she is a little shaken up and has sustained a blow to the head, but the doctors have said she should make a full recovery," said Hannah.

"Thank goodness for that, how did they find her so fast?" asked Clayton.

"I think the owners from the public house you stopped at gave a description to the police about the vehicle used to abduct Jess. A National Trust night security guard found it abandoned during his night patrol. North Yorkshire constabulary told me that Jess was still asleep in the van and she did not witness what happened to her abductor. The paramedics sedated her before transferring her to the ambulance," said Hannah.

"Thank God, she'll be all right," said Clayton.

There was a brief moment of silence before Clayton said, "Talking about being okay, how is Michael? They told me he was struck by the abductor's vehicle."

"Michael is here at Saint Francis. I'm afraid it seems his right knee has been completely shattered, he'll be on crutches for a while, and it's too early to say if he will have any long-term damage, but he definitely won't be walking the beat for a while put it that way," said Hannah.

"Gordon Bennett, you two make a right pair; him with his knee and you with your ankle."

"Yeah, I'm thinking of investing in Hims & Hers wheelchairs," retorted Hannah.

He managed to produce a half smile just as Hannah's face

139

became ashen as she said, "This is with my CI cap on. I've just spoken to the chief commissioner of North Yorkshire Constabulary, and he has said that they are launching a murder enquiry because the main suspect in the abduction has been found in tatters with his head in one field and his body in the woods in a place called Fountains Abbey in Rippon.

"Bloody hell! I suppose it's too early for suspects," said Clayton.

"Yes, from what I can gather, sharp knives, possibly swords were used in the attack. Not sure how many people they are looking for, probably more than one judging by the severity of the attack," said Hannah.

"Well, whoever he or they were, I owe them a drink. At least they got that bastard before he could… I don't even want to finish that sentence," said Clayton.

"I know some things don't bear thinking about." She stood up to leave. "North Yorkshire constabulary will be in shortly to get a statement from you." A quizzical look spread across Hannah's face as she said, "What did you do, Clay?"

"I don't remember much at all. I remember that I wanted to catch up with that bloody van, I knew I couldn't catch up with it on foot but to be honest I wasn't thinking clearly, probably why my jacket was discarded, and the stress may have made me delirious. Anyway, thanks for the 'heads-up', Han. Speak to you soon when Jess gets here," responded Clayton.

"Yes, I'll catch up with you soon, for now get some rest, I'm sure that the White Rose constabulary can wait a few hours, I'll have a word with them," said Hannah as she closed the curtain that surrounded his bed and walked out of his private room.

Clayton lay back on the hospital bed as Hannah's footsteps died away and an awesome realisation hit him 'that the werewolf could track down killers.

The Werewolf could track down killers when it could sniff and taste blood of the perpetrator. The possibilities that this opened up was immense. How was it possible? Could it be that the werewolf's blood lust and fury could be used for a positive purpose; could be used to help serve the public? Help clean up society by clearing the rats and vermin from society. The werewolf could be used to kill people who deserved to be killed: murderers, rapist and child killers. With just a taste of the offender's blood it could deliver some fear and terror that the criminal scum have been dishing out. A pang of guilt invaded Clayton thoughts; how could he frankly be condoning Capital Punishment? The counter argument also entered his head: if you live by the sword, so shall you die by the sword. Surely it was better for werewolf to rip apart criminals rather than innocent law-abiding people.

But for this to happen it must have something to hunt. If the werewolf is not to attack random people it must have a focus. It must hunt out his prey; use its hunting and tracking skills to fight for its blood reward. Clayton whispered to himself in a moment of clarity 'the only thing that the werewolf wants more than killing is the thrill of the hunt'.

Year 1986

Part Three: The Left-Handed Butcher

Chapter 23
Kristina Evans

The autumn moon hung low in the early evening sky. Its light helped to silhouette an abandoned tractor against the dark green rolling farmland. Between the multitude of green hues from the tree canopies and the extremely steep sheep grazing field stood a solitary crimson figure. The figure was completely out of place. Kristina Evans stomped her worn red stilettos and lit up her third cigarette within the past ten minutes. It was the only thing she could do with her hands to keep them from going completely numb on this particularly cold October night. She was a lady in her late twenties but appeared older due mainly to her lifestyle choices and her daily struggle to keep her head above sinking debt.

Damn cops, she thought. They had driven her into the middle of bloody nowhere to pick up the dregs of business. The police had called for an immediate wholesale curfew after the latest girl had been found dead. Not just murdered but butchered, cut up beyond recognition, according to the other shit scared girls.

Sharon Lowe 'Shazza' was her name. She was a newbie on the game scene, not cut out for this kind of life, she wouldn't say 'boo to a goose' which was strange really because she heard she was quite handy with her fist. Even so she was still a 'Newbie' she wasn't experienced enough to be able to read the punters to separate the sugar daddies from the shit-bags. That was the one thing Kristina prided herself on, the ability to spot danger before she got in any.

Due to the greater police presence in Oldham Town Centre, Kristina had to leave the hustle and bustle of the late evening bargain shoppers and the early drinkers to find just one more punter before calling it a night. Jonathan was almost eleven now and probably in bed watching 'Worzel Gummidge' that he taped off the telly. He always enjoyed Worzel even though he had to read the subtitles from page 888. His deafness had not stopped him enjoying the things that hearing kids did. He had to grow up fast to keep up with the other kids and now he was proper Mr Independent. But still Kristina didn't like to leave him for too long even if he was adamant that he wasn't a baby that needed looking after. To be honest, over the last few years he looked after her more than he should. Making her breakfast when she had just one too many bottles of vodka. Cleaning and tidying-up when he knew the social workers were coming around again to check on him.

Jonathan had to put on a brave face after a rough couple of years with that incident outside the bank and losing his great grandparents, who were killed on Crompton moor.

If Kristina was being honest with herself, it wasn't just Jonathan she was concerned about. She had felt differently about prostituting herself since the murders started just over two years ago. She had always known that every time she went with a punter it was a risk, but lately the 'Left-handed Butcher' had put the fear of God into all the girls. Gloria the 'Mother Hen' was the oracle when it came to prostitution she knew everything because she had been doing it since 20 BC (Before Colour).

"He ain't even coming anywhere near us girls, Bolton yes, Blackpool yes, Bury yes and Burnley too. Maybe he only goes to places that begin with a 'B', so we are probably fine here in

144

Oldham, right?" said Gloria half-jokingly the last time all the girls were together.

That perceived crumb of comfort was now well and truly shattered. Shazza was an Oldham girl and was also her friend and now she was lying on a mortuary slab somewhere because of that bastard, the Left-Handed Butcher. Kristina thought all these sick-oh always had to have a tabloid name to sell papers because nothing shifts papers like a psycho wielding a butcher's chopper. The newspapers probably knew more about him than the useless fuzz. She felt a slight pang of guilt thinking that because they weren't all useless some were kind but she was never going to be a charity case.

The police, through the media, had given the public a limited amount of information about his appearance and what to look out for; bushy beard, gapped teeth, slight to medium build. A light brown Fiat Argenta which they were keen to trace. This was all they had on him; how could he always be one step ahead of them. *Was he really a master criminal or just a lucky shit by always escaping capture?*

She shuddered deeply when she thought about him. But then firmly shook her shoulder length red hair with her sharp fringe. No, shudders were not going to help pay the rent, or buy her Jonathan new trainers and shudders were definitely not going to pay for her Benson & Hedges cigarettes with menthol filter card. In a nutshell, shudders wouldn't keep the wolf from the door.

As time passed, the passing traffic or trade in Kristina's case had become sporadic, now nearly every car was a taxi taking inebriated people back home to sleep it off, or to Manchester for even more revelry. She felt a strange mixture of relief and disappointment when she finally decided to give up for the night and made her way home before Jonathan fell asleep. Anyway, punters would probably not bother to consider a B road between Huddersfield and Oldham as a major red-light route. It is not as if she could advertise it in the latest issue of the 'Yellow Pages'. Due to a madman killing prostitutes we have relocated to the 'Park Inn' pub car park between Crompton Moor and Dunwood Park, I'm sure that would definitely raise an eyebrow or two.

She closed her long leather coat which concealed her red, velvety figure-hugging mini dress. It was a relief to have the coats insulating warmth once again as she tied the leather straps together and began pacing towards her home. She had only walked for a few moments when a brown Fiat car pulled up in front of her. It stopped half on the road and pavement. As she walked adjacent to the driver's door the man in the car slowly wound down his window.

"Hi love, are you after business tonight?" asked the man, who spoke with a very soft local voice.

He sounded like a stiff breeze would blow him over. Kristina felt that he was the kind of guy that she could handle if things got out of hand. And anyway, she had her pepper spray in her handbag as backup. She noticed that he had four scratch marks just above his beard line on his right cheek like he had cut himself shaving. This was kind of odd because he had a brown bushy beard.

"Yes, I am looking for business but I've already clocked off for the night so it will cost you extra," responded Kristina, in a nonchalant tone.

"That's okay. I've got money," said the man.

She waltzed round to the other side of the car and jumped in and closed the door, her previous fear had dissipated. She smiled; after all, she was going to get paid and a lift closer to her flat so less distance to walk, a win-win situation.

The man turned to her and said, "I've never done this before, what do you recommend?"

He had a shy, sheepish demeanour with his black leather coat completely zipped up.

"That depends how much you've got on you and what you fancy," declared Kristina.

She rubbed two fingers with her thumb in the universal sign for money.

"I've got money, but just want a blowie," said the man.

"That's my specialty." She laughed. "Drive around the corner and stop in Dunwood car park, it should be dead at this time," she said.

The couple drove the two-minute journey with no small chit-chat, Kristina commented on the weather but the man did not feel like speaking. *He must be very shy,* she thought. The slightly battered brown Fiat was the only car in the car park which was next to the closed down Dunwood Café. The man turned off the engine and turned to face Kristina.

Instinctively, she bent her head down and reached over to undo his fly.

He held up his hands and said, "No, no, please, not here. I don't want to make a mess in my car; let's go into the woods."

Both the Fiat Argenta's occupants quietly got out of the car and walked into a secluded spot in the woods, which was covered on all sides by thick trees with low hanging branches good shelter from prying eyes. Once the couple entered the small clearing, she automatically dropped to her knees and started to rub the man's crotch area while beginning to unzip his fly. After a moment or two, she lifted her head and said, "Don't worry, love, I'll get you hard."

"This is how I get hard, bitch!" screeched the man.

And with that, he produced half a brick from out of his jacket pocket and struck her on the side of her head. The blow sent her slumping to the ground. As Kristina fell, the man kicked her in the eye so hard that she completed a full roll and ended up face-down in the dirt, leaves and twigs. She could feel herself fading in and out of consciousness as her left eye had already started to close due to the extreme swelling. Dark blurred images were all Kristina could make out. She had lost all thought of what had happened. All that went through her mind before she lost consciousness was, *Jonathan, please know Mummy loves you, Mummy loves you, Mummy loves you...*

She didn't have any awareness of the man as he walked slowly towards where she lay. He carefully pulled out a large butcher's chopper with a light grey wooden handle and a dirty rusty blade from a plastic bag carried inside his jacket pocket. He then pulled back his right jacket sleeve and exposed a smiling 'Jack Nicolson' tattoo on his forearm. The woods were deathly quiet apart from the railway track that ran adjacent to the park and rattle of the last train of the evening as it made its way back to the train depot in Manchester.

A glint of moonlight reflected on the rusty blood-spattered blade and also briefly exposed the man's fixed toothy grin and his vacant evil black eyes, void of sympathy. A close by branch broke but that could not distract him from his lusting for death. The man slowly limped and knelt down beside Kristina's comatose body, he gripped the chopper with both hands in readiness to strike her exposed neck. Then with an inhuman spasm, he thrust the chopper into the air.

Chapter 24
Magnolia Tree

Clayton Rudd got up with a slight jolt as his brain registered the drone of his telephone ringing next to the bed. The constant din in his ears eventually woke him from his deep slumber. He had been having a nightmare, with faces of fear; faces of pain all covered in blood all screaming, crying and pleading. He wiped his eyes, yawned then stretched across and answered the blasted telephone.

"Hello, Inspector Rudd."

"Clayton, it's Hannah. Please come in, we have just had another killing."

"Okay, I'm on my way," said Clayton

Clayton hung up the phone and lent over to check the time, four-thirty a.m. He didn't like the rude awakening but still was relieved that it wasn't one of his 'phone off the hook nights'. With another giant yawn he dragged his legs over the side of the bed and flexed his tired bones. A quick shower later and he was dressed in his usually grey two-piece suit and on his way to Central Manchester Police station. Due to his house, One Heather Hill, being exposed on the very edge of Shaw where there was little if any shelter from the Northern wind that blew in from the hilly fields to the rear. He shivered as he walked down the few steps to his waiting car although it was still officially summer but four-thirty in the morning is never pleasant.

His car lit up with a noisy DJ announcement 'and straight

into the top ten is the Cutting Crew with Heart, I just died in your arms tonight'.

Too early for this, he thought and turned the radio straight off again. So, in silence he made the short drive from his home to the Police station in his trusty burgundy Jaguar XJ12 series where he met Chef Inspector Hannah Baker at the entrance to the multi-storey staff car park.

"Hello, Clayton, thanks for picking me up. I wanted to speak to you before we got to the crime scene. Just between you and me, I've been getting heat from above to get results. Things are even getting political now that Margaret Thatcher had to fend off questions about the 'Left-Handed Butcher' at Prime Minister Questions in the House of Commons. Anyway, off the record, I've just had word from our own Maggie who is already at the scene. Her initially assessment is it looks like the work of the 'Left-Handed Butcher'.

"Thanks for the heads-up, Hannah. Let's hope we find something to go on this time," he sighed.

Clayton knew that Hannah was under the most pressure to make an arrest because now in terms of this case the buck stopped with her, because recently she had been promoted again. Hannah and him had joined the police force at the same time and the fact that she had made chief inspector before him had developed to be a touchy subject between the two of them. Now he believed that he had been overlooked for another promotion over the last few years because although he was found innocent of any manslaughter charges, indeed both times, he was found to be acting in self-defence, he was in the force and unfortunately in the police force when mud is thrown, it very often sticks.

"Who has got Jess tonight?" he asked, trying to lighten the mood before they got to the crime scene.

"She is staying at my mum's; Michael is away for a few weeks on the golfing holiday, the one that he had to cancel when he injured his leg," answered Hannah, as she pulled on her seat belt across her chest and lay her handbag on her lap.

"It doesn't sound like much fun hobbling for eighteen holes."

"Chance will be a fine thing; he's going to hire one of those golf carts. Anyway, all he cares about is making sure his follow through is straight and true,"

"Look at you, the expert, I never imagined you as a golf widow. So, are things going well with you and Michael?" asked Clayton.

"Not too bad, he was a bit ratty when he was on crutches but he is back at work now. He won't be running any marathons for a while still but as long as it doesn't affect his backswing, he's okay. I've had him helping out with operation 'Magnolia Tree' staking out popular red-light districts," replied Hannah.

The car's dashboard heater hummed as Hannah warmed her hands on the gentle blowing fan and said to him, "Head to Bishop's Park we had it cordoned off at two-thirty hours. When we had a report of a deceased female found in the wasteland just near the car park."

Clayton's burgundy Jaguar approached the crime scene just as the first light of day shimmered off the misty hills and a desolate golf course. He knew that the area was well known for dogging and other undesirable activities. When he pulled up to the blue & white police tape and slowed down, he flashed his badge and parked his car just outside the cordon off area. They both stepped out of the car and crouched under the tape. They were met by Margaret Hurst the senior forensic pathologist for Greater Manchester who wore a full-length forensic scientist jumpsuit and carried a clipboard under her arm.

"Hello, Maggie, please take us through what you already know," asked Hannah as both herself and Clayton put on their own protective clothing.

"Caucasian female, cause of death severe blood loss from major trauma wounds," answered Margaret.

"Did we have a confirmed ID on the deceased?" asked Clayton.

"Yes, Inspector, we found her handbag at the scene; her name was Sharon Lowe a local girl from Royton, East Oldham," replied Maggie.

All three of them walked closer to take a look at the dead girl.

Margaret continued to fill the other two in on her findings. Her remains were spread over a 4-metre radius; she was only partially clothed; her coat had been removed. The deceased was very nearly decapitated her throat was hacked at. There are also several wounds to the chest area and both legs. She has had her left hand removed in the assault. The attack seemed to fit into the pattern of a frenzied sustained assault all except the concentrated severing of the left hand.

Maggie explained that on first impressions it appeared that her injuries were caused by a large blade probably a chopper or a machete. None of them at the scene said the words but they all knew it was the work of the serial killer in the midst 'The Left-Handed Butcher'. The attack had all the hallmarks of the butcher; semen left at the scene, the deceased hacked up beyond belief and the left hand severed, but this time unlike all of the others, the hand was found at the scene.

For two years now, the butcher had cast a shadow all over the counties of Lancashire and Greater Manchester. No woman felt safe. Sex workers seemed to have taken the brunt of the killings, but all women were held by the fear of the darkening streets. It was the fear of the unknown, he could have been your husband, father, brother, best friend or son.

Chief Inspector Baker and Inspector Rudd who had been assigned to the case a year ago went into the makeshift tent while Maggie verbalised her findings into her trusty a mini Dictaphone.

The first blow seemed to have missed its intended target judging by the tear to the coat just on the victim's shoulder. The disturbance to the foliage and the marks on the muddy grass seemed to indicate a violent struggle. The victim's left-hand had been severed just below the wrist. The hand is adorned with various rings including a Whitby Jet stone set in a gold band and a large green emerald ring on the thumb. The hand is pale and had lost most of it colour but appeared to have fresh blood on each chipped fingernail. She then pressed pause on her Dictaphone.

Clayton's heart leapt in his chest at these words. Is it possibly they could finally have a sample of the killer's blood! Maggie stopped the tape and turned to the two detectives and said, "It seems that Sharon tried to fight off her attacker and may have scratched him, it looks like she put up quite a fight," said Maggie.

"When will you know if the blood on the fingernails is our murderer," asked Clayton.

"I will be able to match the blood samples and give you a definitive answer within the next twelve hours," she replied.

"Thank you, Maggie, please make the bloods your main priority," said Clayton.

"What about the tyre tracks? Do they match the ones from the previous attacks?" inquired Hannah.

"We are taking photos and a cast at the moment. It is too early to say if they belong to a Fiat Argenta but again I will give you an answer ASAP," replied Margaret

The police already had a witness to the crime, a fellow sex worker and Sharon's friend called 'Gloria'. She was found near the scene bawling hysterically. Gloria was the one who discovered the body, and in all possibility disturbed the perpetrator making him flee the scene. She was taken to the station and after she had time to calm down, she made a statement about what she saw. She said that she didn't get a great look at Sharon's client but saw that he was driving a small light brown beaten up old car.

Early the next day Chef Inspector Hannah Baker called a meeting to discuss the latest developments in the case. The briefing room was full of police detectives who were seated around a large wooded oval table and uniformed officers who were standing by the walls or gathered around the water cooler. Hannah brought the meeting to order and addressed Inspector Clayton seated to her right, "What is the latest information we have on the case of the Killings around Greater Manchester and Lancashire? Clayton, do we have a photo fit of our perpetrator?"

"We did manage to get a photo fit of our suspect from 'Gloria'. It was dark when she saw him but at the moment it is the best we have got. I will circulate the image to the press tomorrow morning."

"Thank you, Clayton, Constable Ford could you please tell us what is the latest on the search for owners of Fiat Argentas?" asked Hannah.

"I have located and eliminated seventy-four cars that are registered in the North-West region. There are another two hundred and sixteen to go," said Constable Richard Ford who was the only member of the uniformed policemen to be sitting around the table.

"Thank you, Richard. I will make some more resources available to you to help you eliminate the rest of the Fiat Argenta owners as quick as we can. Now, Maggie is it still too early to identify the blood sample found at the scene?" asked Hannah.

"We should know the results by tomorrow morning, ma'am," replied Margaret Hurst while referring to her typed notes.

"Okay team, let's review what we already know and make sure that we haven't overlooked anything.

"The first known victim was Ellie Tierney a young lady known to be prostituting herself for only a few months, she was found on waste land near Bolton Wanderers Football Stadium. Her body was found by 'Fletch', a local woman of no fixed abode who was scrumping for fruit on the wasteland bushes. Estimated time of death was 2 a.m. on Saturday, 15th December 1984.

"The second victim was reported missing on the Wednesday, 3rd April 1985 one Bethany-Rose Beckford. Her family didn't know that she was working as a sex worker. Her body was discovered three days after being reported missing on a patch of wasteland on the outskirts of Blackpool. We have some information which the press is not privy to. We analysed the CCTV footage taken from the Woolworths store on the high street and we can see that the last positive sighting of her as she got into Frank Simpson's purple Ford Capri. Frank is known for being a pimp with a large illegal cohort of ladies spread over the Greater Manchester and Lancashire area as well as being a member of the notorious Simpson gang. Frank has a history of using extreme violence against women both in his private life and I use this term loosely, his clients. We have so far been unable to

155

locate Mr Simpson to bring him in for questioning.

"The third victim, Holly Barnes, was found in an underground passageway linking Bury Market to the public car park on Thursday, September 11th, 1985. Again, she worked in the sex industry.

"The fourth victim, Sangeeta Kaur, from Burnley, again another sex worker was found on Thursday, 19th December, 1985 on the embankment of the M6 motorway.

"Then there is a gap of over eight months between the fourth and fifth victim. Why was there a gap? Was he out of the country? What was different in that twelve-month period? After all, serial killers don't just take a break!

"Finally, the most recent and fifth victim was Sharon Lowe found in Oldham on Friday, 13th August, 1986. Once again, she was a sex worker. From what we know, Sharon was into her fitness and self-defence. She was a black belt in Taekwondo and it appears she may have injured our suspect."

"Clayton, can you continue?" said Hannah.

"Yes, it seems that our offender doesn't stick to one location but travels around mostly Greater Manchester and Lancashire. Only the police are aware of his modus operandi. Ideally, we don't want to reveal any more information to the general public for the following reasons, we don't want to spread blind panic and we definitely do not want any copycat killings. Unfortunately, the person who found the body of Ellie Tierney a homeless lady known as 'Fletch' went to the paper and told them about the missing hand. That's why we now have the nickname 'The Left-Handed Butcher' to deal with. But butcher is an appropriate name sadly, the killer chops at the body in a random fashion but one thing that is always the same, he hacks off and removes the victim's left hand. This latest attack is the first time the left hand was recovered at the scene.

"Really disturbingly, all of the victims except for the last were mutilated and sexually assaulted post-mortem."

Hannah Baker then continued, "There is a certain amount of frustration building up; we need to catch this guy soon. Already New Scotland Yard have said that they will be sending up a number of detectives to micro-manage our investigation, so make sure we cross every 'T' and dot those bloody 'Is'. They want to know why we haven't made any arrests, and why we are always chasing shadows. Why it is that operation 'Magnolia Tree' didn't give us any new leads? We were hoping to catch him in the act and yet we could only arrest men for refusing to pay the ladies and causing a disturbance. At first, we were insisting that the girls needed to at the very least go out in pairs so they could watch out for each other.

"I am now suggesting that we ask all sex workers to stop completely until we catch this guy."

Hannah sighed, and said almost under her breath, "Why is it when we think that the net is closing in, he finds a way to slip through?"

She then sat up straight in her chair and in a loud clear voiced addressed everyone in the room.

"Finally, we will catch him with good old fashioned police work, he has been lucky avoiding us, but sooner or later his luck will run out."

Chapter 25
Strangeways Prison

The prison van rounded the corner after it left North Manchester General Hospital. Soon it meandered its way through the barbed wire street near Strangways Prison. The white Group4 van was in the middle of an armed police escort which consisted of an unmarked black BMW 3 series car at the front and a dark blue one at the rear. Inside the heavily reinforced prison van sat Leroy Simpsons. Both hands cuffed to the interior wall of the van and his legs were also shackled together. He was joined in the van by two heavy set armed security guards, one guard whose forehead glistened with a sheen of sweat sat chomping on bubble gum that periodically he would blow into a bubble that exploded over his face and left a blue tint to his bearded double chin. His already large creased white shirt struggled to contain his considerable frame as the shirt buttons were hanging on for dear life. It is fair to say that the shirt touched where it fit. Every slight bump in the van wobbled his large belly that in turn sent a wave of motion up his torso to his chest. Resting on his 'Des' name badge was the handle of his large wooded baton. Every so often, he would slap it into his palm in a threatening manner and periodically smile at the Leroy.

Leroy rocked slightly in his seat as the van manoeuvred over another speed hump.

"Oi, Meathead, how about loosening these bloody handcuffs! It's cutting off the blood to my bloody hands!" Leroy shouted.

The large security officer who was in mid-bubble blowing swallowed the sticky blue mess and looked across at Leroy.

"Since you asked so nicely, you can piss off! You've just had your pampering session in the hospital for your poor tummy ache," responded the security guard.

Leroy raised his middle finger as far as the shackles would allow. "Sit on it, fatty"

The guard grunted and looked over at his colleague who was more interested in emptying the content of his nose as he dug his chubby fingers deeper and deeper looking for crusty green gems. His arm was resting on the butt of his automatic rifle.

"A right bloody charmer we've got here." Both the guards smiled at each other.

The other guard who hadn't spoken yet Troy said, "One of the notorious Simpson Brothers, so feared, so dangerous but now without his brothers, he is just a pussy!"

Leroy made an action as if he wanted to punch the security guard that had just made that comment.

"Get me out of these chains and I'll show you who's a pussy!" shouted Leroy.

Both security guards looked at each other and laughed. The van continued on its way which took it passed an industrial estate close to the Boddington's brewery. An aroma of roasting hops filled the North Manchester air. Maybe it was the distraction of the pleasant aroma in their nostrils but no one seemed to notice the black Land Rover which secretly followed the convoy. No one took a blind bit of notice of the dark blue ford Capri which came in the other direction, or the two masked figures crouched down behind the parked cars.

There was an eerie silence in the air as the convoy passed

the two hidden figures. Even a passing chatty magpie held its breath in anticipation. Then the world exploded in a blast of noise. The two men jumped up from their hiding spot and emptied their automatic rifles into the four occupants of both escorting cars and the driver of the van. None of the four-armed guards in the two escorting cars even had a chance to raise their firearms; the attack was so swift and so brutal. The Land Rover that initially kept its distance all of a sudden roared up the road and smashed the tail of the rear escorting vehicle and rammed it into the two parked cars. It then rammed into the back of the Group4 van and buckled both rear doors. The Land Rover reversed and the two masked armed men pulled the doors back even further with a crunch of dented metal on metal. Shots were fired from inside the van as the bullets ricocheted around the metal interior. One of the masked men had executed the two guards shooting them at point blank range. As one of the guards lay dying, he had just enough strength to pull his trigger one last time and killed the other masked man with a shot to the chest.

Another man jumped out of the dark blue Capri with a pair of bolt cutters and freed the restrained Leroy Simpson. The three men jumped out of the van and into the waiting car which screeched off up the road closely followed by the busted-up Land Rover.

"Yes, yes, fucking. Yes," shouted Frank still holding his automatic rifle.

"Boom that was quality, those pricks didn't know what hit them, who was that guy who took a bullet," said Leroy.

"Just a fucking junkie Cock-Eyed Colin, I still can't believe I brought that liability along, I said he would get fifty notes for a professional job, but he was hardly a professional, dumb shit leaving a dying man with an automatic rifle in his hand. Bloody thick! Only good thing was that he took the bullet instead of me," said Frank.

Leroy then turned to Frank as the driver drove like a bat out of hell, as the car left smoke trails in its wake.

"Frank, did you get the information?" asked Leroy.

He smiled and said, "Hell yes! It took some doing but enough money can buy any information."

He threw an envelope over to Leroy.

"Get in tonight, we get even with that shit of a policeman and avenge our dear brother Billy," shouted Leroy.

Then in quieter tone he turned to Frank and said, "Frank it will be just you and me, we will take care of this situation, and we alone will have the pleasure to end that pig's life. I don't care if he dies slowly or in a hail of bullets all I care about that he knows we have avenged our dear brother. Frank once we dump this car get the purple Capri and we will go and pay him a little visit. I can't rest knowing that he is still breathing."

"No problem, Leroy, I had a feeling you would want to sort out this situation straight away so I've already gathered a selection of firearms for your perusal," laughed Frank.

The envelope was clenched tight in Leroy's fist as a wide mischievous smile spread on his face. There was an address written on the envelope with one name underlined at the top CLAYTON RUDD.

Chapter 26
Gloria

Clayton started on his night shift and picked up the out of uniform PC Richard Ford; they drove into the middle of Oldham to patrol known red light area looking for any suspicious activities. They were especially looking out for any light brown Ford Argenta Cars. The sun was low in the sky as it approached dusk. Clayton's burgundy Jaguar pulled up alongside a BP petrol station next to the dim, quiet streets of an industrial estate. 'Operation Magnolia Tree' had scattered most of the prostitutes from their usual haunts but this industrial estate was still a popular spot for the diehard ladies. The two police officers soon noticed two ladies touting for business.

"Look, guv, there are a couple of ladies we should have a word with," said PC Richard Ford.

"Yes, Dickie, let's have a quiet word," said Inspector Rudd.

The first lady was a large black woman who was dressed all in black. She wore fishnet tights, black high heel stilettos, tight black mini skirt and a leather jacket with a fluffy trim around the collar. She had large permed black hair and massive hooped earrings that a large Jack Russell dog could comfortably walk through holding a bone in its mouth. The woman's lips were painted with luminous mauve which jarred against her dark brown skin. She stood with a handbag on her shoulder keeping an eye out for any potential clients. Clayton recognised her as Gloria who was the eye witness to the Sharon Lowe murder.

Her friend was a few years younger and he instantly recognised the woman's face. It was Kristina Evans. For some reasons not quite clear to himself, he felt a pang of guilt. This woman's son had effectively saved his life and she was selling her body. He knew that he couldn't help everyone in a desperate situation but did he owe her more than a thank you bunch of flowers and a happy meal for Jonathan. Surely, he thought he could have done more but what? If he took a keener interest in her welfare several alarm bells would have been rung and his superiors surely would not be approving.

Clayton and PC Ford stepped out of their unmarked Jaguar and approached the two women. As they did, a car a that had slowed down all of a sudden sped up and disappeared around the back of the nearby Werneth train station.

"Oh brilliant, there goes another customer, because here comes the cavalry. You two couldn't look less like cops if you tried," shouted Gloria.

"Oh, shit Glo, that one is Clayton Rudd the policeman that was involved in that incident a couple years ago with Jonathan," whispered Kristina to Gloria

"Sorry about that, we tend to have that effect on curb crawlers," said PC Ford, as they got closer to the two women.

Clayton and Kristina didn't say anything at first just ignored each other with a strange atmosphere between them, like bumping into your ex-girlfriend on a night out and not knowing whether to speak to them or ignore them.

"Well, are you going to give me the twenty pounds that you chased away?" said Gloria to constable Ford as he got within ear shot.

"You know with the current climate we have strongly asked that all soliciting activities be halted," said Constable Ford.

163

"Oh, yeah and are you going to pay my rent, get my fix and stop my old man from giving me a hiding when I come home without anything to show from my night's work?"

"You know that we have set up emergency measures as part of Operation 'Magnolia Tree'," said Constable Ford.

"I don't want a bag of rice and some bloody carrots!" said Gloria with disdain.

During Constable Ford and Gloria's heated exchange Clayton and Kristina started to have their own conversation which began much more sedate.

"Hello Kristina, how have you been keeping?" asked Clayton. Even as the words left his mouth, he knew it wasn't the most sensible question he had ever asked. She walked a few steps away from Gloria and Constable Ford.

"I've been okay, just getting by you know how it is," replied Kristina.

"I'm sorry, I never knew you worked the streets, if I had known I could maybe have helped out," replied Clayton.

"Help me out, Clayton, I'm not a charity case, yes earning money like this was never on my career path but at least I'm earning my own money and standing on my own two feet. I don't need a man to sweep me off my feet and be my knight in shining armour!" she said.

"I never said anything about charity," said Clayton.

"Then why do you want to help me out there are hundreds of girls that work the streets, what is so special about me, do you feel a sense of duty because of what Jonathan did," said Kristina.

"No, nothing like that," said Clayton

"Then what is it, please tell me, what it is?" asked Kristina

"I care about you! I care about you okay, there is no other reason, it is not a sense of duty or guilt it is just that I like you and seeing you working the street is like a kick in the gut that's all," said Clayton.

"You care about me, why me, what's so special about me? I'm not really the kind of girl you can take home to Mum," she said.

"My mum has passed so that's not a problem," said Clayton.

"You know what I mean. I've not been in a relationship with a man since Jonathan's dad and he shat on me from a great height," replied Kristina.

Clayton did not respond to her comment because both of them became acutely aware that constable Ford and Gloria had ceased their conversation and were staring at both of them.

"Okay, miss, please remember to take extra precautions and should you see a man driving a Fiat Argenta matching this description please call the number on the card, thank you for your cooperation," said a sheepish Clayton and then walked back to Constable Ford and Gloria.

The two policemen then walked back to their car without speaking. As soon as they both got in Clayton's car, they could see the two ladies walk off past 'Patel's News' towards Oldham bus station.

"Maybe they are catching the evening bus home," said Constable Ford.

"Or may be just moving to another patch," said Clayton.

"You seemed to know the other woman, Inspector," said Constable Ford.

Clayton said, "I do Constable, or should I say I thought I did... I thought I did."

Chapter 27
A Purple Ford Capri

Frank Simpson sat in the passenger seat of his own purple Ford Capri no matter whose car it was Leroy was always the driver. With a turn of his wrist, he turned the ignition key and suddenly the souped up engine died along with Bob Marley's smooth vocals mid chorus of 'Redemption Song'. The car was parked halfway down Heather Hill Road with a view of number 1, Clayton Rudd's home.

"We'll just chill here for a bit and wait until it gets a little bit darker," said Leroy.

"Yeah, no worries. Well, it looks like he's home; there's a motor on the drive," replied Frank.

Both men sat in the rapidly cooling car with fully loaded Uzi 9mm submachine guns on their laps.

"You had the choice of ammo. Why did you want to bring the Uzis? Are you expecting a whole gang up there?" asked Frank.

"I wanna make sure that this time when I finish with him, they'll have to mop up what's left, I don't just want to kill him but completely destroy him, so there isn't anything to bury," said Leroy.

Frank gently nodded his head, and said, "He lives in this big old house on his own, he must be worth a few quid too, could be a good score."

"I don't give a shit about all of that... don't forget he killed our kid. Anyway, let's sit tight for a bit and get our game face on," said Leroy.

Both men sat and waited for the skies to darken so they could approach the house without being detected. The clouds overhead thicken as the sky slowly lost it verve and the shadows lengthen.

"Okay, bro, let's go bring the bolt cutters for the back door," said Leroy.

"Yeah, will do," said Frank.

"Whoa, chill for a minute, look," said Leroy.

Both men sank down again in their seats as a beige Mini City 1000 car slowly passed their vehicle and parked outside Clayton's house. A woman in her 30s got out and walked up the few steps to his front door.

"Shall we come back, it looks like he has got company," asked Frank.

"Nah, bru, we'll deal with her too," said Leroy.

The men waited a few minutes as the woman engaged in a conversation with Clayton on the door-step. The conversation was prolonged and unexpected by the woman as she stood there holding a bottle of wine. Leroy and Frank then seized their opportunity to get into the house. They both pulled on their black balaclavas and quietly crept up to the house, kept low and when they could see that the couple were distracted, they attacked.

Leroy instantly ran up the short flight of steps to the front door and smashed Clayton's left eye with his gold-coloured knuckle duster, knocking him to the floor in the hallway. Then Frank bundled the woman into the house and slammed the door, dragged the woman with one hand around her throat through to the living room and held her mouth closed with the other hand. Leroy proceeded to punch Clayton repeatedly again and again in the face while he was on the ground, eventually knocking him unconscious. He then held the woman still as Frank taped her mouth shut and pulled out the cable ties to fasten her hands in front of her body and then tied Clayton's hands behind his back. After both were secured, Frank started to have a look around the house and straightaway found that the book case had been moved to reveal the hidden staircase leading to the underground bunker. He tentatively explored the hidden rooms, before he ran back full of excitement and shouted to Leroy, "Yo, this guy has got an underground safe room. He must be loaded. Let's wake him up and tell us what he is hiding down there."

"I'm still not bothered about his money, I'm just gonna off him," replied Leroy.

"Yeah, we are going to off him, but this might be a big score too," said Frank.

"Okay, let's take him downstairs and see what he is hiding. It may be a bit quieter down there anyway for when we plug them," said Leroy.

Frank then grabbed Clayton under his arms and dragged him down the stairs whose back thudded against each of the forty concrete steps on the way down before he was dragged and dumped in the middle of the main bunker room floor. Leroy then pulled the woman down the stairs by her hair and threw her down onto the concrete floor a couple of yards from Clayton.

The act of being dumped on the floor along with being slapped mercilessly slowly brought Clayton round as he opened his swollen right eye as his left eye was swollen shut and felt the pain from his bloodied broken nose.

"Who are you? What do you want?" asked Clayton as one of his front teeth fell to the floor, followed by a stream of a mixture of saliva and blood. The brutal assault to his face had left him almost unrecognizable from the previous thirty minutes.

Leroy the taller of the two masked men then squatted down until his face was level with the now seated Clayton and pulled off his black balaclava and revealed his face. Clayton could see through his right eye that it was Leroy Simpson.

"Hey man, look at me, motherfucker, you know who I am. I'm the motherfucker that has been itching to get you ever since you off'd, my bro!" shouted Leroy right into Clayton's face.

A shudder of shock quivered through Clayton's body as the recognition of the man's face registered with his brain.

"Surprise, bitch, did you think you saw the last of me in that courtroom?" said Leroy.

"How... did you—" stuttered Clayton.

"How did I manage to find you? Can't find the words now. Shitting it, are we! Did you think you could blow away me younger bro and just walk away scot-free, without any type of retribution! You're bloody mad if you think that, now the last thing you're going to see is my face when I blow you away," shouted Leroy.

Clayton did his best to speak through his swollen bleeding lips. When his voice came, it was quiet and extremely hoarse.

"I know you have beef... with me, but please let her go, she has... nothing to do with it," he pleaded.

"Nah, man, I can't do that, she's seen my face," said Leroy with a wry smile on his face.

"What do you have stashed down here, piggy? That's a pretty thick door, you definitely want to keep people out," said Frank.

"It's to keep... me in, you'd... better go now before it's too... late. Please just... go and lock me in. You don't have much... time!" pleaded Clayton.

"This guy must be trippin' if he thinks we are just going to

169

leave him here," said Frank.

Leroy then stuck the barrel of his Uzi 9mm into the pus-filled swollen face of a stricken Clayton and said, "There is no way you can talk yourself out of this sticky situation you're in."

He then moved the handle of the gun close to Clayton's swollen eye then smashed him in the face. He lost his balance and fell on his back. As the back of his head thudded onto the cold concrete floor, he let out a cry of pain and started convulsing and tried to break free of the cutting cable ties around his wrist with violent thrust of his arms. His good eye closed as pain swept through his body.

"I've had enough of this bullshit," said Leroy and stood up from his squatting position lifted his Uzi 9mm and pulled the trigger for all of three seconds. Believe it or not, those three seconds were enough to discharge thirty plus bullets straight into Clayton's chest, exploding his heart, liver and other vital organs across most of the floor and half-way up the opposite wall. Over the hysterical screams of the lady, Leroy approached the oozing mess of a corpse and stood over it lowered his Uzi 9mm and said, "This one is for Billy!" and unleashed another twenty bullets into Clayton face and head and sent his exploded brains sliding across the room, joining his organs splattered on the far wall.

Chapter 28
The Vault

It was the night of another full moon and Clayton began his now monthly ritual. He could feel the coming of the change. It was something you could feel but not describe like how you know you have two pieces of A4 paper between your fingers but can't describe the differences in thickness. He made sure that the front and back doors of the house were locked, and then glanced outside the living room window down his small isolated street. He only had a handful of neighbours on Heather Hill Road and it looked like one of them had a visitor or a new car. There was a purple Ford Capri parked at the other end of the street. A little too garish for him, he thought, *Oh well, each to their own.*

He then opened the secret passageway and was about to descend when the doorbell rang.

Maggie Hurst drove the twenty-minute journey with all the trepidation of a high school girl asking a boy for a dance. She knew she was just being silly, Clayton had been her colleague for four years now and she had never even bothered to look twice at him. But there was something more attractive about a middle-aged man who was unattached and could commit to a relationship. She had enough of being used by men that said they want to be with her, but were just using her for her body or her disposable income. Indeed, she was quite a catch, that's what she kept telling herself. And beside she did have a genuine reason to turn up unannounced at his house. She could now confirm that the blood found on the severed hand did indeed belong to their prime suspect and the bottle of wine was just to soften the blow of disturbing him off-duty.

Maggie walked up the short flight of steps to Clayton's front door and rang the doorbell with a mixture of dread, excitement and feeling a little foolish. She twisted the bottle of 1982 Shiraz nervously in her hands making it squeak as she waited for any signs of life, behind the locked door. She then saw a figure move behind the frosty glass. The bright colours all danced around until the door opened and Clayton Rudd stood there in a multi-coloured dressing gown, full of 'Marvel' comic book characters, spider-man swinging through the air and hulk smashing.

"Oh hi, Maggie, this is a surprise. I was just going for a shower," he said.

"Oh sorry, I knew I should have phoned in advance, but I had already left the office when I thought about coming over to give you an update on the blood sample. So, the blood found on the fingertips almost certainly belonged to the killer," she said.

"That's really great news, Maggie, but what's with the wine?" said Clayton.

"You got me, ha," laughed Maggie.

Suddenly, an uncomfortable silence fell upon the two of them. Until finally, Clayton spoke, "Maggie, I am truly touched and I would love to share a bottle of wine with you, but now is a really bad time."

"I don't mind waiting while you have a shower; it'll give me a chance to wipe the brightness of your dressing gown from my head," said Maggie.

Clayton laughed nervously. "No, really, Maggie, now is a really bad time—"

He had barely finished the word 'time' when the gold

knuckle duster came over Maggie's shoulder and caught him square in the left eye. The force of the knuckle duster dislodged his eyeball and it swelled up almost immediately blinding him in that eye. Then a shorter man grabbed Maggie by the neck and put another hand on her mouth to stifle her screams of horror. The taller man then kicked Clayton as he fell in the hallway of the house. Another series of violent punches rained down on his temple and face until one finally knocked him unconscious. When he was down the two masked men then preceded to tie up Maggie. She feared for her life and did not give the balaclava wearing men any more reason to hurt her. So, she tried to cease her screaming as they sealed her mouth with a strip of grey gaffer tape. The shorter man motioned to the taller man and said, "Shall I gag him?

"Nah, there's no point, his talking days are over, just tie him up," said the taller man. The shorter man then had a look out of the living room window.

"I don't think anyone heard us, it's like a ghost town out there," said the shorter man.

Who then started to have a look around for anything worth stealing, he inspected a few ornate vases and collectable figures of 'Rocky balboa' and 'Clubber Lang' from the new movie 'Rocky III' but nothing of much value. Then he spotted the bookshelf that had been moved away from the wall exposing an illuminated stairway.

After a quick look down he came back and shouted up to the taller man.

"Yo, bro, check this out this guy has got some sort of secret passageway. He might be stashing the good stuff down there."

He then proceeded to drag the unconscious body of Clayton down the full four flights of stairs, dumping his body in a heap on the cold concrete floor in the dimly lit main bunker room just in front of the opened vault door. The taller man then dragged Maggie kicking and moaning into the underground bunker by her hair and threw her to the floor not far from Clayton.

"Wake him the fuck up, there is no way that he gets to die in his sleep," shouted the taller man as the shorter man proceeded to slap Clayton's face until he groggily opened his right eye.

"Hey man, look at me, motherfucker, you know who I am. I'm the motherfucker, that has been itching to get you ever since you off'd, my bro." And with that the man pulled off his balaclava and looked right into Clayton's face.

"Surprise, bitch, did you think you saw the last of me in that courtroom? Hey Frank, did this guy actually think we wouldn't track his arse down!" said the smiling Leroy.

The late evening full moon gradually appeared from behind the smoky clouds in the crimson sky, just as Leroy smacked Clayton straight in the face with butt of his firearm.

The time for conversation had finished when suddenly Leroy opened fire with his Uzi 9mm and splattered Clayton's torso across the room covering the whole of the wall in blood. Maggie, who was sitting on the floor at the same level, screamed as the bullets flew in the air and deflated Clayton's body. The room echoed with thunderous thuds as the bullets left the chamber, screeched and ricocheted off the concrete floor. The ear splitting bullets were no match for the screams of Maggie who's gaffer tape had come away from her mouth with the continued movement of her lips and allowed her to wail at the horror she saw. She did not stop screaming as parts of Clayton's inners were splashed against her face and onto her bound hands.

Just when Maggie's horror level was at ten, she watched aghast as the man now stood over Clayton and fired another twenty bullets or so into his skull. When his brains had stopped sliding across the floor, the man turned and slowly walked towards her towards her as he began to reload his Uzi.

"Now there is only one loose end to tie up," said Leroy.

"Maybe we can have a little fun with her before we send her to meet her friend," suggested Frank.

"Yeah, man, I like white meat, hold her down for me," said Leroy.

Maggie started to scream again as the two men's intentions became all too clear. She didn't notice that Clayton's blood that had splattered on her face and hands had now disappeared. None of the three people in the room saw how the blood once splattered thinly across the width of the room had now gathered in a shallow pool on the floor. Just like spilling water on a waxy table cloth and then playing the footage in reverse. Every bit of blood, brain, skull, sinew, mucus and muscle slowly slid and made its way back to its source. Slowly, blood re-entered Clayton's veins, bone matter miraculously fitted back together without any joins. Within a minute, Clayton Rudd was completely restored. For the briefest second, he appeared as if he was just sleeping on the floor, but after that brief second, his eyes opened and his previous blue eyes were now yellow with black oval pupils. His teeth suddenly sharpened and dark black hair sprouted, as his bones contorted and stretched. A wolf's muzzle forced its way out of his face, but it didn't produce its usual howl; instead, all its fury seemed to be building up for an explosion of rage.

The shorter man Frank Simpson held down Maggie's shoulders as Leroy ripped open her pink blouse. Maggie's violent left and right jerking motion suddenly stopped when she saw the werewolf slowly stand up behind Leroy. The horror in her eyes didn't alarm Frank or Leroy as she held that horrified look from the moment they held her down.

A giant backhand swipe from the black werewolf knocked Leroy clean off Maggie and sent him hurtling into the opposite wall. The crash against the wall knocked the wind out of him, as his Uzi 9mm also went skating across the floor and ended up wedging under his shoulder. Dazed and confused, he lay on the floor trying to come round as the air was shattered by the constant thuds of Frank's Uzi.

Frank saw the beast sideswipe Leroy and instantly opened fire sending forty nine mm bullets crashing into the werewolf's black hairy body. They only just slightly bloody his skin before being expelled and the bloody indentation healed instantly not even scratching its skin. The bullets just fell to the floor in a compacted smoking mess like a pile of cigarettes behind a bus shelter. The beast then took a giant step over Maggie as Frank stopped to reload his Uzi. The second cartridge was in and instantly he started to off load into the snarling snout of the growling werewolf. These bullets like the previous chamber penetrated the skin slightly before being dismissed and the thick skin instantly healed. Frank screamed as the bullets flew and thudded against the oncoming beast. Eventually the pull of the trigger was discharging fresh air after the final bullet left the smoking barrel.

With one man lying winded and another occupied with the werewolf Maggie saw her chance to escape. She slid back on her backside with only her legs for propulsion over the course, gritty concrete floor. She could see a groggy Leroy as he got to his feet, stumbled and slipped trying to get to the vault door. He was just about to get out of the room when Maggie pulled her legs clear of the door and reached up high with her still bound hands and pressed the dusty red button. The huge door then swung closed and in doing so violently knocked Leroy back into the room with a high pitch squeal, a thud, then silence.

Maggie could see the live pictures on the TV monitor as Leroy thrust at the door in a vain effort to get out. She could also see in the background Frank who still wore his balaclava backing away from the werewolf that was Clayton two minutes earlier.

Frank reached into his inside pocket for another redundant round of ammunition but he was out anyway. He was left with one simple choice; fight or flight and seeing that bullets were discarded like wedding confetti he didn't fancy his chances so he started to run for his life. He tried his best to sidestep the beast with a drop of his shoulder but he was like an overweight Sunday league footballer playing with a hangover and the beast was far more agile and with his giant claw swiped the fleeing Frank, slicing him into almost five separate pieces that fell to the ground like some kind of macabre human sushi. His steaming mess of a body twitched and spread as the werewolf took a giant step over his body and walked towards the frantic Leroy who was like a rat caught in a trap with no escape.

Leroy also emptied the rest of his ammunition into the approaching werewolf's torso again the inadequate bullets didn't even break the creature's giant steady stride. Eventually, he threw the useless empty assault rifle at the beast's head, striking him on the right eye but the beast barely even blinked. The fight or flight decision was now faced by Leroy and he already knew that the flight option had gone. So, he came out swinging but his reach was no match for the reach of the werewolf who grabbed the onrushing Leroy, picked him up and ripped him in two, sending his lower torso and legs to the left and his upper torso arms and head to the right. The werewolf then howled as Leroy's entrails flopped down his shoulders and chest.

177

Maggie watched on the TV monitor as the beast thumped against the door again and again and again as it tried to get out but the door held firm. She watched until exhaustion and fatigue finally got the better of her and she fell asleep on the cold concrete floor with her hands still bound together.

Chapter 29
Tattered Dressing Gown

Clayton opened his blurry eyes. They took a minute or two to decipher what they were trying to focus on. It could have been a piece of trampled heart or a punctured lung. Whatever it was it was splattered on the floor and less than six inches from his face. He peeled his face off the ground and broke the cold gooey strands that tried to bind him to the concrete floor. When he stood up, he noticed that he was completely naked, his marvel dressing gown was now on the floor in tatters and covered in human goo. The locking door mechanism had already unlocked the door and it was now wide open. As he walked to the entrance of the room, he saw Maggie fast asleep, gently snoring with her knees bent, leaning to one side. He covered his manhood and tiptoed quietly up the stairs to have a shower and break out a length of dental floss.

Maggie Hurst woke up with a start as she felt the slight pull on her wrists.

"Woo, let me go, woo, no," shouted Maggie.

"Relax, Maggie, it's just me. I'm just cutting off these cable ties," said Clayton.

Maggie looked at Clayton with stunned shock on her face for more than three minutes as fresh tears rolled down her cheek as she shuddered and kept opening and shutting her eyes in disbelief.

"You died, I saw that man fill you full of holes," gasped Maggie.

"Yes, and I would be brown bread if they would have come on another night and not on a full moon," replied Clayton.

"I can't believe you became that thing, that beast... How, when did all this happen," asked Maggie.

"I've been like that for just over two years now, ever since the night Griffin was killed. I couldn't say anything at the time because who would believe me, but Griffin was killed by a werewolf and before I shot the beast, he had already clawed my back and infected me with the werewolf's blood thirst. You yourself said that you saw silver in the bullet found at the scene where Ken Goodwin the park ranger died," said Clayton.

"So every month you have been out slaughtering innocent people?" asked Maggie.

"Hardly, I've been locking myself away here every full moon and as you can testify, not even the raging werewolf can break through that door," he said.

He leaned over Maggie and cut off her cable ties, finally freeing her hands.

Maggie gingerly sat up and pulled off the piece of gaffer tape that still clung to her right cheek and rubbed the red scratch marks on both of her wrists. Clayton helped her to her feet.

"Do you want something to eat or freshen up?" asked Clayton.

"That can wait, firstly what are you going to do with the bodies?" asked Maggie.

"I don't know; this is the first time I've had to deal with any bodies. Last time, I just left the scene, I mean this is the first time," stumbled Clayton.

"What do you mean last time? I thought this was your first

killing on a full moon?" asked Maggie.

"Yes, that's right. This is the first time that the werewolf has killed on a full moon. I changed in the middle of the lunar cycle once, when Jessica was abducted. I just wanted to save her by any means and that included killing Barry Stone and I think my own bloodlust summoned the wolf and brought on the change," said Clayton.

"Yes, how could I forget that case? Jessica was found at the scene in West Yorkshire. I was brought in when they found hair fibres on that tartan blanket from the missing girls from Greater Manchester. The initial crime scene investigation team said he was found near his van, minus his head," said Maggie.

"Talking about bodies, what we are going to do with these, are we going to call it in?" said Clayton.

Maggie thought for a minute with her head in her hands then said, "Clay, you know as well as I do that there is no way we can explain this. Who's going to believe that you came back from the dead to slaughter these two people? Anyway, as far as I'm concerned, you didn't kill those two men. It was the werewolf, you were just a vessel for it. I'm not totally without blame. Yes, I was acting in self-defence but by closing the door on those men last night, I basically sentenced them to a death," said Maggie.

"What do you have in mind, Maggie?" asked Clayton.

"Let me get a few chemicals from my car. I'll soon sort this place out. Don't forget, I know what to look for and I also have access to the incinerator," said Maggie.

Clayton let out a slight fake laugh and said, "Note to self, never upset you, they will never find my body."

Maggie tapped Clayton's chest with her finger and said, "That's right and don't you forget it."

Chapter 30
The Hand

It had been nearly four weeks since Clayton plucked up the courage to speak to Maggie again. He knew things would be just a little awkward between them for a while. Let's face it, they had a hell of a lot to digest over the previous few weeks. Miraculously, Leroy and Frank's purple Capri car turned up a week later, completely burnt out on the edge of Saddleworth Moor just off the main road to Holmfirth. The police indeed investigated the disappearance of Frank Simpson when his wife broke cover and contacted the police to say that he had failed to return home. Technically, Leroy was missing too, but it is hard to report him as missing when he was on the run from the authorities. The word on the street in Manchester was that they were taken out by a rival gang and that their bodies and possessions would probably never be found.

Clayton buzzed the intercom to the Forensic Science Pathologist Department in the centre of Manchester. The large brown 1930s Art Deco building stood out against the surrounding modern architecture. The ledge of the building barley stopped the rain from hitting his face, he did consider getting out his black statesmen like umbrella from out of his Jaguar boot, but it was only just spitting when he had parked up.

"Hello, Inspector Rudd, to see Margaret Hurst," said Clayton.

"Thank you, Inspector, please push the door," said the voice through the intercom.

The loud buzzer echoed over the traffic noise as Clayton pushed open the door and stepped inside the old building that looked like a high school from the 1960s. The corridor was totally wood panelled and smelt freshly polished. The 'Mr Sheen' smell in the air was mixed with a faint odour of chlorine which always reminded him of his local swimming pool.

"You know where you're going, Clay," came the receptionist's friendly voice from a little way down the shining corridor.

"Yes, thanks, Laura," he responded.

He entered Maggie's laboratory and instantly he knew she was right in the middle of some kind of forensic deduction as several items were laid out on a large stainless-steel table. She had the severed hand of Sharon Lowe being preserved in what looked like a small witches' cauldron with the smoky dry ice floating out across the table. She also had the deceased woman's clothing laid out on the table as if she was wearing them. Her dress was neatly spread out with her stockings below along with her high heeled shoes. The top of Maggie's thick black rimmed glasses popped up over the far side of the table.

"Hello, Clayton, I was beginning to think you were avoiding me," said Maggie as she measured an incision hole through the front of Sharon's black leather jacket.

"No, I wasn't avoiding you, just really busy, you know what it's like," responded Clayton with an awkward smile on his face. Now it was his turn to be shy and coy as he was trying to find the words to get something off his chest.

"Maggie, I have had something on my mind about our Left-Handed Butcher case and I think there may be a chance for us to get this guy once and for all," said Clayton.

Maggie stopped measuring the rips in the leather jacket and looked at him. "What did you have in mind?" asked Maggie.

"I told you about the werewolf killing Barry Stone when he abducted our Jess. What I didn't tell you is that myself and Barry fought before he got away. I broke his nose and some of his blood spurted on my jacket. My theory is that when I changed into the werewolf it somehow used its advanced sense of smell and tracking skills to isolate the bleeding, fleeing Barry and killed him and saved Jess and also satisfying his blood lust. I think if it has someone to hunt, it will not kill indiscriminately and we can use it," said Clayton.

"So, what are you saying?" asked Maggie.

"I think that if the werewolf had a sample of the perpetrator's blood sample, it would use it to track down and kill the Left-Handed Butcher and you have a sample of his blood on the severed hand of Sharon Lowe," said Clayton.

"I can't believe what you're saying, you want to kill someone in cold blood!" said Maggie.

"The werewolf has already killed people; Barry Stone and the Simpsons brothers," said Clayton.

"Yes, but killing Barry saved Jess and the Simpson brothers, at the very least, you were acting in self-defence. Who made you judge, jury and executioner? If the werewolf tracks down and kills him, then there will be no trial, no cross-examination and no explanation for loved ones or possibility of closure! We are in the law enforcement business, doesn't he deserve the protection of the law!" said Maggie.

"Maggie, you yourself examined Barry Stone's van and you found hair fibres from each of the murdered girls on his blanket and their fingerprints were also found in the van, not to mention their scratch marks. I have stopped him killing again. Sometimes, the end justifies the means, so you can save me all your politically correct rhetoric, I'll tell you this that when Jessica was abducted, not once did I think I hope he gets a fair trial after he strangles my daughter. No, I wanted to kill him before he could harm one hair on her head. I told you, I think that is why the beast came out even when it wasn't a full moon to satisfy my own bloodlust. Anyway, have you never heard of the saying 'live by the sword and die by the sword?' Even the Bible says, 'An eye for an eye, a tooth for a tooth," said Clayton.

"The Bible also says, 'if you strike me on the left cheek, offer the right'," said Maggie.

"Why don't you go and tell the family of Sharon Lowe to turn the other cheek!" said Clayton.

"Whoa, that's not fair, Clayton," said Maggie.

"I'm sorry, Maggie, we could keep on arguing but what we have here is a classic ethical dilemma in which every available choice is wrong. So, all I'm saying is that I don't want to break the news to another family saying that their mother, sister, wife or daughter have been brutally murdered if there is just the smallest chance that I could do something to prevent it."

Maggie looked directly at him and said, "Sorry, Clay, I haven't got time to continue our little chat at the moment. I've got to get this trolley back to the evidence vault."

Then she systematically started to fold the clothing up and carefully placed them back into transparent evidence bags. Next, she carefully took the severed hand and that too went in her large flat based trolley that was parked next to the table. Clayton knew that his words had fallen on deaf ears as he watched her load up the evidence trolley his head flopped down in despair. Maggie came over to him and put her hand on his back.

"Sorry, Clay, I would have loved to help you if I could; now as far as I'm concerned, we never had this conversation—" She paused for a moment. "I would say see you later, but seeing as it's a full moon tonight, I guess you're busy... We never did open that bottle of wine," she said just before she walked out of her laboratory.

He heard the door swing close and steady tap of Maggie shoes clip clop down the corridor until they could no longer be heard. He tried to get over his sense of disappointment. He raised his head slow and noticed that something was left on the desk right in front of him. It took him a minute to identify what it was because his eyes were just a little misty. In a plastic bag with a giant evidence sticker saying 'Sharon Lowe' were the remains of a severed hand.

Chapter 31
The Werewolf

Clayton put down his 'Presto' carrier bag with its special content inside on a coffee table in his front room and sat down on his sofa. It was already getting dark and the moon would be at its zenith within the next hour as he could already feel its pull. The enormity of what he was about to do was only just hitting home and he knew that if things went to plan he would be waking up and the Left-Handed Butcher would be spread across a good couple of acres. The time for cold feet had long since passed; especial thinking about the risk Maggie had taken for this opportunity.

With a slight tremble of his index finger, he pulled down *The Strange Case of Doctor Jekyll and Mr Hyde* book and the bookcase sprung forward. The faint smell of bleach still lingered as he descended the stairs with the 'Presto' carrier bag and set it down on the floor outside the automatic door. Then walked up the long thin tunnel that exit was concealed behind bushes, shrubbery and a light spattering of wild poppies. He spun the squeaky wheel that opened the heavy submarine style door and winced as the frosty wind blew up the side of the hill and whistled down the tunnel, bringing in the drizzle from the fresh crisp night.

Clayton stumbled as the odd raindrop found its way down the tunnel and made it slippery. *Would it have killed Uncle Patrick to have installed a handrail?* I guess 'Health & Safety' wasn't that big in Nuclear Bunkers in the 1960s. The funny juxtaposition made him smile as he regained his footing. His brief, light hearted nature soon dissipated as he saw the carrier bag flapping in the breeze.

The halogen strip light above his head flickered as it powered to full brightness. He took the hand out of the plastic evidence bag which was in the 'presto' bag and placed it on the floor of the hallway. Then he got undressed and folded his clothing and placed them on the floor in the underground bunker. As he stood completely naked, the cold breeze brought the skin on his arm out in goose bumps which lasted for all of ten seconds until he started to change. His bones stretched and twisted, growing to eight feet tall. Black hair started to sprout out all over his body, his feet and hands turned into claws. Muscles had grown from under his skin until what stood in the hallway of the bunker was an eight feet tall muscle bound werewolf. It bent down and picked up the severed hand, held the dried bloody fingertips to its muzzle and sniffed the blood then stuck out its tongue and tasted the blood. Then it let out a massive howl as it dropped the hand to the floor. Now it had the taste for blood. It turned and bolted up the secret exit and out through the bushes onto the side of the hill.

The werewolf breathed in the still night air and smelled and tasted a multitude of different aromas, but his heightened senses were locked into one in particular, one smell amongst the millions; incredibly, it was The Left-handed Butcher's. His Fiat Argenta snaked its way down Buckstone Road, which ran parallel to Crompton Moor, and that's exactly where the werewolf ran. Through the farmer's field next to Clayton's house over the stream and the adjacent forest, up the sharp incline until it reached Crompton Moor woods. The smell of its prey was getting stronger as the Fiat Argenta came closer and closer. The car's headlights shone through the woods as the werewolf zigzagged through the trees. The Fiat had gone past the point of the road where it met the woods. So, the beast missed its chance to crash into the car and devourer its occupant. It then turned and ran full pelt straight down the steep valley side keeping close to the wood line just behind St Saviour's church while the hymn 'Walk in The Light' drifted up the hillside, as the car's red rear light disappeared down the winding road.

It could tell that the car stopped for a brief moment and was now on the move again and this time there was also a female scent coming from the car.

The car drove down the road and turned left, the blood of the Left-Handed Butcher still registered on all of the werewolf's senses. It got more intense as the car rounded a bend and came back slightly and parked up in a sandy car park in a deserted Dunwood Park, next to the closed down cafe. The werewolf leapt across the road into the wooded area adjacent to the gentle slow moving brook, but there was nothing slow about the werewolf as it stretched every muscle and sinew to close the gap on its prey.

It could sense a change in their location; they were no longer in the car for the scents were coming from deeper into the woods. Suddenly, it heard a dramatic change in the two people's heartbeats. First, the man's accelerated to a highly excited state, and the woman's beat a rhythm of extreme fear, then dropped as if she were unconscious.

At that moment, the Rochdale to Manchester late evening express train came dashing down the track completely blocking the hurtling werewolf from the park. All of a sudden, there was a new scent in the air. The woman was bleeding; this knowledge did something inside the beast. It instantly reacted as it leapt over both sets of train track, the hurtling express train, the high razor sharp fence and the dense line of bushes landing straight on the other side on the grass in Dunwood Park. With another leap, the

189

werewolf crashed through the trees and saw the man kneeling over the woman with a chopper held high in the air as it briefly gleamed in the moonlight. Again, the werewolf leapt through the air just as the man brought the chopper down towards the woman's neck but instead buried it deep in the outstretched left forearm of the werewolf. The man fell back and the appearance of the werewolf seemed to shake him out of his murderous trance.

The beast howled with rage as it pulled out the bloodied chopper out from his left forearm with its right claw. Instantly, the wound healed even before the discarded chopper had time to hit the forest floor. It took one giant step over the unconscious woman, and growled menacingly at the shocked man who was scuttling on his backside away from the towering beast.

"No, no, no, no, noooo," screamed the man.

But the werewolf bent down and picked up the man by his left leg and held him outstretched upside down. A gasping wheeze was the only thing audible from the man as he struggled to catch his breath. Then suddenly, the werewolf with its right claw slashed the man, sending half of his jacket, his wallet, head and most of his vital organs flying through the air, clear of the woods and car park. His organs splashed down on the side of the park's café, splattered against the brick wall, then trickled down onto the plants and flowers below. The next swipe separated the man from his left arm as the remains of his body just flopped to the ground, leaving the werewolf still holding his left leg which he tossed to the left and it came crashing down just next to the now empty train track.

The werewolf threw its head back and howled at the slowly setting moon. Lights began to turn on in the bedrooms of the few adjacent houses that bordered Dunwood woods. It turned and leapt into the woods and disappeared. The woman on the floor slowly gained consciousness as the police sirens cut through the night as they rapidly approached.

The werewolf's bloodlust had been satisfied and it returned to the still open hatchway and started to slide down. At that moment, the moon began to fade and lost its power over the beast. Instantly, the beast began to limp as its body started to retract and contort at the top of the tunnel. His black hair retracted and its muzzle shrunk away. At the bottom of the slide came out a naked, steaming and bloodied Clayton. He stood still for a moment or two before gathering his thoughts, closed the escape hatch and collected his clothing. He collected the severed hand to return to Maggie and went for a shower.

Clayton got dressed after his shower into his dark grey work suit. Then he sat down to wait for the phone call that was sure to come at any moment. And then one and a half hours later it came, his hand trembled slightly as he reached to pick up the phone receiver. He cleared his throat, took a deep breath and closed his eyes.

"Hello, Inspector Rudd here," said Clayton.

"Good morning, sir, this is PC Richard Ford. I'm sorry to call you so early but there seems to be a major development in the Left-handed Butcher case. We have a witness that has survived an attack and there is also one male fatality at the scene. Chief Inspector Baker is already there and she has asked if you can join her ASAP."

"Thank you, Constable Ford, please tell her that I'm on my way."

Year 1984

Epilogue
'All Work'

Clayton had barely finished off the last of his Shiraz when the doorbell rang. He opened the front door to find of all people in the world Michael Baker, his ex-wife's new husband, standing in his porch way carrying two shopping bags.

"Oh hello, Michael, this is a surprise," said Clayton.

"Oh, hi, Clayton, Hannah asked me to get a few things for you. She said that Maggie had said that you have been moping around at home for the last few weeks and she was worrying about you," said Michael.

"You can tell Hannah and Maggie that I am fine, but thank you for the groceries. I hope you didn't go to any trouble," said Clayton.

"Oh, no bother, it's nothing really, just some bread, milk, bacon and a four pack of Hofmeister the bare essentials, no pun intended," joked Michael.

"Follow the bear, I get it. Once again, cheers, Mike," said Clayton.

Michael handed the bags of groceries over as Clayton asked, "How is Jessica doing?"

"She's fine. She and Hannah have gone down to London for a bit of mother and daughter time, wasting money on Oxford

Street no doubt. Anyway, I've got a few days to kill before they get back, so I might check out that new movie 'Ghostbusters' at the Roxy," said Michael.

"Nice one, well thanks again for the bread and milk and enjoy the movie," said Clayton as he said bye to Michael.

He watched as Michael climbed into his dark blue BMW 7 series, drove down the hill and disappeared around the corner.

Michael's car travelled through the heart of Manchester until it stopped outside a garage lock-up. Twelve aluminium garage doors facing each other all numbered. Having parked his car on the adjacent street, he strolled into the garage lock up and opened shutter number eleven. He walked into the garage and a few moments later, the growl of an engine echoed in the tight space and the darkness outside. The opened garage door illuminated from a car's headlight. Slowly, a dark brown Fiat Argenta car came out of the door just a few metres before it stopped and Michael jumped out to shut the aluminium door and lock its central handle with his key.

Michael's new form of transport then headed towards the M62. He no longer had the inkling to sit for a couple of hours and waste his precious time alone at the flicks. So drove for fifty minutes or so and exited the M55 and entered Blackpool's red-light district. He slowly cruised around until he saw a woman in her early twenties getting out of a purple Ford Capri. He watched the black driver of the car tug on a cigarette as he drove past Michael's Fiat Argenta going in the opposite direction. The pretty blonde-haired girl with black roots coming through sauntered up the now abandon street and leaned over to the driver's window as Michael slowed down. "Are you a visitor here? Fancy a lovely Blackpool style Night? Remember, love, what they say, what happens in Blackpool stays in Blackpool," said the women with a cheeky smile.

Michael nodded and smiled too, and showed his wide toothy smile.

The woman jumped in his car asked him to flick on the interior light.

"What's your name?" Michael asked.

"Bethany Rose, but you can call me Beth if you like. Have you got a light, sweetheart? I keep telling myself to cut down, it's costing me a fortune.

Michael stretched over with his left hand and pressed down on the tiny silver wheel which instantly emitted a glowing red circle to light Beth's cigarette. As he stretched over, his jacket rode up slightly exposing a smiling Jack Nicholson tattoo.

"Oh, I like your tatt," said Beth.

"Thank you, I had it done to remind me of something."

"Oh yeah, what is that?" asked Beth.

"All work and no play makes Jack a dull boy," said Michael.

Beth tried to smile, but it did not reach her eyes. The engine croaked when the car slowly set off heading due east towards a piece of wasteland where privacy will be required.